A GOOD CHANCE

THE SIREN ISLAND SERIES, BOOK THREE

TRICIA O'MALLEY

A GOOD CHANCE
The Siren Island Series
Book Three

Copyright © 2020 by Lovewrite Publishing
All Rights Reserved

Cover Design:
Damonza Book Covers
Editor:
Elayne Morgan

To my friend, Margaret. May you continue to bloom.

"It's time, my little seed. The rain is here, the spring has come. Break your shell and sprout."
– The Dark Knight

"*J*'m sorry, but – you did what?"

"I signed up for a reality show on an island in the Caribbean. Well, like a competition, actually."

"And why would you – or anyone – *do* such a thing?" Avery pushed her glasses up on her face and pinched the bridge of her nose, a dull ache beginning to pound in her head. It was inevitable, because her twin sister Ruby came with a side of headaches, Avery thought, and eyed her sister warily. She might as well have been looking in a mirror, aside from the fact that Ruby had recently added blond highlights to her auburn hair and sported a small beauty mark above her lip. Otherwise, they were identical twins, both strong, lean, and with a massive head of riotous curls that had encouraged more than one man to make lewd comments about the red-headed sisters.

"Oh, come on," Ruby pouted, pushing her thick

lower lip out and bracing her hands on her hips. "Where's your sense of adventure?"

"Right where it should be – with reasonable things like ziplining in Costa Rica or discovering a new restaurant in Times Square."

"Like you would *ever* zipline in Costa Rica." Ruby rolled her eyes and crossed the bedroom to start rummaging through Avery's closet, a habit that was long ingrained but had never ceased to put Avery on edge. It wasn't that she minded sharing her clothes; it was that Ruby pulled them all out of order and staunchly refused to put them away, leaving a heap of discarded dresses and shirts on Avery's pink tufted velvet chair, her one concession to whimsy in her bedroom.

"I might. You don't know that. And if I do, it's not going to be with a bunch of cameras trained on me so my terror can be publicized to the whole world."

"The winner gets $100,000," Ruby said, pulling a brilliant green shirtdress, spotted with white lilies, from the closet and holding it in front of her. Avery hadn't even worn it yet, but she was so shocked by Ruby's comment that she ignored Ruby when she tossed the dress over her tote bag.

"Are you kidding me? For going to a Caribbean island? Is this even a real show? That's an insane amount of money." Avery mentally calculated all the bills she could pay off – from student loans to her outstanding medical bills from a traumatic accident a few years ago.

"See? Not sounding so stupid now, is it?"

"But what do you know about this show? How did you even get on it? How do you win money? Do you really have to be on television?" Avery peppered her sister with questions, pushing her notebook aside and giving Ruby her full attention. Ruby flopped onto the bed, crossing legs clad in screaming yellow skinny jeans, and flipped her hair over her shoulder.

"The island is called Siren Island, and from what I've read they have a lot of mermaid myths on the island. How cool is that?" Ruby asked, avoiding the questions. Avery was well-versed with Ruby's tactics, and just stared her down.

"Okay, fine, it's called *Swept Away,* and I applied for it months and months ago. I actually totally forgot until, like, a month or so ago, when they called me in for casting and I went through more rounds of interviews. Then I signed all the contracts and it's set to start soon. You win money if you and the bachelor choose each other, and you have to make it through certain challenges. It's kind of like a dating game and an island survival game in one."

"Island survival game." Avery immediately pictured spiders and cockroaches crawling over her legs in a sandy tent.

"Yup. But like… posh, you know?" Ruby tilted her head and gave Avery a blinding smile, which immediately set off all of Avery's internal warning signs. Ruby was about to ask Avery to do something for her. A very big something.

It had been like this their whole lives, Avery

thought. She'd followed her dazzling sister through a series of adventures as they grew up. Well, more like she'd tried to stop Ruby from being so reckless, and had always been her clean-up crew and moral support when things went up in flames. Ruby was impulsive, and dove head-first into any fleeting whim she had, while Avery made lists of pros and cons and consulted others for advice before making a big decision. It suited her well as an engineer, but was often cause for arguments between the sisters. Mainly, Ruby arguing that Avery needed to lighten up a bit.

The last time she'd taken that advice, however, she'd gone kayaking with her then-boyfriend, Mr. Outdoors Colorado Man, who had inadvertently taken her down a Class V rapids. Avery had been rewarded with several broken bones, a month-long stay at the hospital, a week in a medically-induced coma, more medical bills than she cared to think about, and a now ex-boyfriend. If she'd just followed her gut and taken the less risky approach, she'd have enjoyed having a picnic by the river and watching the birds fly by above. Instead, with Ruby's words in the back of her head, she'd broken out of her comfort zone – and had broken her body in doing so.

"What do you want?" Avery said, reaching back to massage the tightness from her neck.

"Well, you see, when I signed up for the show, I hadn't met Zane yet." Ruby pouted once more, and Avery almost rolled her eyes. Zane was Ruby's latest fling, an Australian surf instructor. She'd heard all the details about him, including his infamous moves in the bedroom, for two months now.

"Right, and he probably won't like you going on a show to hook up with some dude," Avery said, shrugging a shoulder. "Simple. Don't go on the show."

"Erm… not that simple," Ruby said, smiling that bright smile at Avery again. "They've already got my picture up, social media profile, website…all the stuff. And I signed contracts."

"So? Go on the show then. I'm sure Zane will understand. He seems pretty adventurous."

"Yeah… about that." Ruby bit down on her lip again and Avery wanted to scream.

"Just say it. I know you're easing me into it, but I swear to god, Ruby, I've told you a million times – it's easier to just rip the Band-Aid off. What do you need?"

"See… that's the other part. Zane and I just bought a world ticket."

Avery just looked at her sister blankly.

"A…"

"A world ticket. It's this open-ended plane ticket where you can travel the world in one direction and hit a bunch of countries so long as you use it in six months."

"Okay, and? So go after the show."

"I leave next week," Ruby said, the look on her face both sheepish and excited.

"Wait… what? You're leaving next week to travel the entire world? For months and months? And you're just telling me now?" Avery shrieked, "What about rent? What about our apartment? What about your houseplants?"

"You pay most of the rent, because I'm never here," Ruby pointed out. "And I always kill the houseplants anyway."

"What about your job?"

"I can always pick up another marketing gig, Avery, it's fine." Ruby shrugged.

"But… what about me? You're just going to leave me?" Avery asked, her eyes round in her face. Despite their differences, the sisters had an unbreakable bond and as much as Ruby annoyed Avery, she'd still miss the hell out of her sister.

"I'll be back. It's okay – this is good for you, Avery. You need to break out of your comfort zone. I'm worried for you… ever since you got hurt –" Ruby's eyes filled at the mere mention of the accident – "you've gone all hermitville on me. You were bad before, but now it's just work, gym, and watching Netflix. You need to be out, experiencing life. You're twenty-seven, not retired. You need to break out of this rut."

"I'm not traveling the world with you, Ruby. I have a job. One that I quite like, actually," Avery said, pushing aside Ruby's comments about her being a hermit.

"I didn't ask you to travel the world with me. Even I know I can't get you that far out of your comfort zone. But you are owed a vacation. You haven't taken one since you started at the firm three years ago," Ruby said, raising an eyebrow at Avery.

"So? I'll take one. Soon. I promise."

"Great! I'm glad you said that, because I need you to take my place on the show," Ruby said, smiling her con-artist smile at her sister. Avery, for once, was left without words, and she stared at her sister with a mixture of panic and anger.

"No. Nope. No way. Never, *ever*, happening," Avery finally said when she could breathe again. "A love show? On an island?" She might as well have said – Smoking crack? With a side of acid?

"You have to, Avery. They can sue me if I don't go on. The contract says so."

"What kind of contract did you sign, Ruby? That sounds like slave labor. Tell them you're sick. That's life. I'm *so* not doing this."

"Please? Just think, you'll be a perfect shoe-in for me. And you could win $100,000. That's enough to pay off all those bills and put you in the clear for your future."

"I think you and I both know the likelihood of me winning an adventure challenge – and a man's heart – on a game show are slim to none."

"You'd be surprised. It's always the unexpected one who wins."

"No, Ruby. A hard no."

"Just think about it. All that money. A vacation in the sun. Cute guys…" Ruby smiled at her.

"Not happening."

"But you never take risks anymore. Is this what you want from your life?"

Avery's mouth dropped open. She was about to protest when she realized Ruby was right. She'd been cautious even before the accident, but after? It had spun her into a life of taking very few chances. Unless, of course, Ruby dragged her into something.

But either way, a reality show was not happening. Going out of her comfort zone was more along the lines of trying online dating or eating at a new fusion restaurant. Going on television? So. Not. Happening.

CHAPTER 2

*S*weat trickled down the back of Avery's neck, even though she'd turned the airplane's air vent on full power. Her hands clutched the armrest as the pilot announced their descent. What had she been thinking to say yes to this? Avery craned her neck to look out the window, noting that she couldn't see anything but turquoise water below. Where exactly was the pilot intending to land this little scrap of a plane?

"It'll be fine. The landing is a bit rocky, but the pilots do this all the time." A breezy blond woman sandwiched next to her on the twelve-seater plane offered her a reassuring smile.

"This is… not in my comfort zone," Avery bit out. That seemed to be the theme ever since she found out about the show. Despite swearing up and down she would not take Ruby's place on this stupid reality show, somehow Avery had found herself requesting time off from work and booking a plane ticket. She was powerless to stand up to her sister – what Ruby wanted, Ruby always got. Avery had resigned herself to the nature of their relationship years ago, but this particular escapade really was off the charts. And, as much as Avery hated to admit it, she did need to be pushed out of her comfort zone. The accident had shaken her so much that she'd become scared to put herself out there. Granted, putting herself out there had looked more like attending a book fair in a little village on the East Coast, not hopping into this death trap that was currently hurtling toward a speck of an island in the Caribbean. But in any event, she was here and there was nothing she could do about it.

"I doubt many people particularly enjoy flying in these tiny planes," the blonde said, having pulled out her headphones and put away her iPad.

"Have you been to the island before?"

"Nope, first time. Though I have traveled a lot in the Caribbean. But I'm here to film a reality show, if you can believe that."

"So am I! And, again, out of my comfort zone," Avery said, and extended her hand. "I'm Ruby – but call me Avery. I go by my middle name." Ruby hadn't told the producers she had a twin sister, and they'd both decided it would be easier if Avery could use her real name; otherwise she'd just be confused the whole time they were filming.

"Hi, Avery, nice to meet you. I'm Cherylynn." The deep drawl of southern Texas tinged her words.

"Nice to meet you. I have to be honest… I signed up

for this on a dare. I have no idea what I'm in for." Avery had decided to tell people she was doing this on a dare in order to explain why she seemed so reluctant. Try as she might, Avery just wasn't one to exude bold confidence and sultry seduction techniques. Ruby had put her on a vicious schedule of watching hours of reality-show love challenges, and it had quickly become apparent that Avery had little in common with the women who signed up for these shows.

"Well, now, honey, you're gonna have yourself a good ol' time," Cherylynn drawled. "Think of it this way – you get to hang out on an island and meet new people. Either way, you win."

"I'll try to keep that in mind," Avery said, clenching the armrest tighter as the plane dipped like they were going over a bump on a rollercoaster. Her stomach rolled, but she forced herself to breathe through her nose.

"Almost there. See?" Cherylynn nodded to the front window where the pilot readied the plane for landing. The airport, with a runway that hardly looked long enough for them to land on, was nothing more than a little yellow box on the side of a dirt strip. Avery swallowed down her fear.

"Why are we doing this again?"

"Because it's an adventure."

"Why do we need adventures? I like being in my comfy pants and relaxing on my couch where I don't have to worry if my plane will stop in time or go shooting off the side of the island into the ocean where sharks will probably immediately descend on us and rip us to shreds."

"My, my. Someone's been watching too much *Shark Week*." Cherylynn pursed her lips. "In any event, we'd be dead once we hit the water so I wouldn't fuss too much about sharks."

"Not helping."

"I'm just saying…"

The plane bumped onto the runway, making a surprisingly smooth landing, and zipped across the dirt strip before pulling to a stop in front of the brightly colored airport. Avery let out the breath she'd been holding. Reaching back, she pulled her hair into a messy bun on the top of her head, already knowing the heat and her hair were not going to mix. At least she'd taken her sister's recommendations and dressed in light linen harem pants and a loose silk tank.

Packing for this trip had been a nightmare.

"No, no, and no," Ruby had declared, diving deep into Avery's suitcases and tossing clothes every which way. As per Avery's usual protocol, she'd started packing as soon as she'd decided to go on the trip, making lists and ordering things like bug spray and first aid kits from Amazon Prime. Ruby had pounced as soon as she'd seen the luggage, and her last gift prior to going on her world tour was to pick Avery's outfits and style her for every possibility. Knowing her sister, Ruby had even made a little notebook with drawings and outfit choices, so that Avery could easily pick what she should wear for each event. Normally, Avery would ignore

Ruby and wear whatever she felt comfortable in. But knowing she'd be on national television had given her pause, and she'd relinquished the styling reins to her sister while compiling lists of survival gear she needed to have to last on the island.

Today's outfit – labeled Airplane Chic – was doing its job, Avery thought, by not making her look like a total schlep as she stepped down the little staircase that folded from the plane. Ducking her head, she tucked herself under the wing and then stood back as they unloaded her luggage.

"Didn't pack light, did ya? Expecting to stay a while?" Cherylynn laughed, her large black sunglasses dominating her face.

"I… I have a tendency to overprepare for things. In the event of emergencies. Like… what if the water supply goes out? I have tablets to purify saltwater. That kind of stuff."

Cherylynn pushed down her sunglasses and leveled a look at Avery.

"If the water goes out, I'm on the next plane home."

"I suppose that's an option as well."

"Maybe I should room with you. It seems like you'll be well stocked in case of emergencies." Cherylynn nodded at Avery's two suitcases and small duffel bag.

"I'm ridiculous. I get that."

"Nothing wrong with being prepared. I'm surprised they didn't charge you more for extra bags."

"They did. But I figured it was worth it. I'll be able to relax more knowing that I have what I need."

"And just what is it that you need, honey?"

"Reassurance," Avery said automatically. She tried to tuck a loose curl back into her bun before they started the haul across the tarmac.

"Type A, huh?"

"Totally."

"Nothing wrong with that. It's best to know yourself and embrace your strengths. No sense trying to change or apologizing for what makes you *you*."

"Thanks, I appreciate that. I hope we'll have fun here."

"Me too, honey, me too. And judging from the looks of it, it's gonna get interesting." Cherylynn nodded to where a group of women, each one more beautiful than the next, huddled together outside the airport. A harassed-looking woman rushed around with a clipboard, ushering the group toward several waiting vans. Avery gulped as she spotted two cameramen already filming. Turning away from the camera, her eyes landed on a man standing to the side, his muscular arms crossed over his chest, mirrored sunglasses shading his eyes. Dark hair curled around his ears, at least a few months past a haircut, and a weathered backpack was slung over his shoulders. He looked coolly confident, as though nothing would shake him, and yet Avery sensed a level of disdain pulsing from him as he eyed the group of women. This was entirely different from the looks the rest of the airport employees were giving the group – wide grins were exchanged between many a man standing nearby.

"Do you think that's the bachelor?" Avery whispered, nodding toward the guy in the backpack.

"I hope not. He looks scruffy." Cherylynn scrunched her nose up.

"You think? I think he looks confident. And annoyed," Avery said, and then felt heat rise in her face as the man in question turned to look at them. Striding over, he stopped just in front of the two ladies.

"Ruby and Cherylynn?" His voice, with just a hint of a West Coast accent, sent a little shiver across Avery's skin.

"I'm Ruby. But I actually go by my middle name, Avery," Avery said, offering her hand and a small smile. The man took it, his touch sending another shiver through Avery, and she mentally kicked herself for staying out of the dating game for so long. There was no reason that a handshake with a handsome man should set her system on high alert.

"I'm Roman. I'm the producer of *Swept Away* and I'll be around the whole time for your journey here. If you have questions or need anything, I'm the man to answer them. See the woman with the clipboard? That's Eileen. Also a valuable resource. She's more bark than bite, but I don't recommend getting on her bad side."

"Thanks, Roman. What do you need from us?"

"You'll just need to speak to the customs agent and then we're ready to go to the villa and go over all the rules. Everyone else has arrived and we're already filming."

"Eep," Avery said, and shot a glance around at the

cameramen. Luckily, none of the cameras were
currently pointed at them.

"You do realize you signed up for a reality show,
right?" Roman asked, accurately reading Avery's terror.

"I do. I just… the reality of it… haha… is a bit
shocking," Avery said, plastering a fake smile on her
face.

"You'll get used to having the cameras there. We
always film for a day of just everyone having fun prior
to getting into the actual show. It gives people a chance
to loosen up and forget that the cameras are watching
them."

"Alcohol helps," Cherylynn piped up, and a smile
flitted across Roman's face.

"It helps to make for good television," Roman said,
and Avery read the warning in his voice.

"Good to know. Okay, off to customs and we'll be
there shortly," Avery said. "Should we put our luggage
—"

"We've already loaded it," Roman said, and Avery
whirled around to see that her bags were gone.

"Jeez, you're quick."

"You might want to pay a little more attention to
your luggage when traveling, if two big guys can
wander off with your bags and you didn't even notice,"
Roman pointed out, and waved them off while he went
to confer with Eileen.

"Yeesh, that was rude," Avery said, annoyed
because Roman was absolutely right. She should always
be paying attention to her luggage when traveling.

"It was. Luckily, he's just the producer and not our bachelor. Could you imagine? He's acting like he's too cool for this or something."

"Or like he has someplace better to be."

"Maybe he does. But this is his job. A little less attitude would be nice."

"I don't think throwing in with a big group of women trying to win a man *and* a cash prize is going to put us in a position where there's 'less attitude' around."

Cherylynn threw her head back and laughed, patting Avery's arm as they waited for customs.

"I'm going to like you, Avery."

"Thanks. I sincerely hope we can be friendly through this."

"It's just a game. Nothing life-threatening."

"Good, I was worried everyone would be awful." Despite herself, Avery turned and looked over her shoulder. Another shiver raced through her when she found Roman watching her – with disdain or approval, she just couldn't tell.

"Nah, it'll be fun. Promise."

Avery wished she could mimic Cherylynn's confidence, but her stomach was in knots. If there was one thing she knew for certain, it was that she did not belong with the bevy of beauties about to board the vans.

Making a mental note to kill Ruby the next time she saw her, she smiled brightly at the customs agent and took a step toward the unknown.

CHAPTER 3

*O*nce again, Avery imagined all the ways she was going to torture Ruby when her sister got back from her world trip. Squished between Cherylynn and a woman who could have passed for a supermodel, Avery felt dowdy, overheated, and annoyed at being out of control. Typically, when she did let herself travel, she had a list of accommodations, hired all her own transport, and knew exactly where she was going. Now, she felt confused, out of sorts, and uncertain about where the vans were taking them. There had been no indication in the contracts where this villa would be set up, and Avery had kept herself up many a night studying the map of Siren Island and using Google Maps' street view to try and find an image of villas big enough to fit all the contestants. Some might call her neurotic, but Avery liked to think of herself as being organized. Or at the very least, prepared. And nothing could have prepared her for what she'd gotten herself into, Avery realized, as the babbling women in the van threatened to overwhelm her with their inane chatter about what were the best shoes to wear on a beach. Didn't these women know that wearing shoes in the sand was all but inviting a sprained ankle?

Cherylynn nudged her and whispered quietly, "You okay?"

"Um, sure? I don't know. We'll see." Avery blew out a breath and offered her new friend a weak smile.

"We're almost there. It'll get better once we're out of the vans and we can unpack a bit, get settled in. You'll feel more comfortable, I'm sure." Cherylynn had obviously already gotten a clear read on Avery's misgivings.

"It looks like we're arriving. Is this the east coast of the island?" Avery craned her neck around to look out the window. "I think it is. Which means, if we're lucky, we'll have good trade winds and fewer bugs."

Cherylynn's eyes widened as she stared at Avery. "You studied the wind patterns?"

"I… um… well, I just read about it in a travel forum is all." Avery felt a blush tinge her cheeks – the curse of many a redhead – and shrugged her shoulders.

"I hate mosquitos." The beauty next to them scrunched her delicate nose and shivered.

"Who doesn't?" Cherylynn rolled her eyes and Avery bit back a smile.

"I agree, they're the worst," Avery supplied before the beauty could get in a huff. If she even had the brains to get in a huff, Avery wondered, while the girl held up her phone and made kissing faces into the camera.

"We're here." Cherylynn nudged Avery as the vans turned onto a dirt road and rolled past several villas – one that had "The Laughing Mermaid" brightly scrolled on a sign above the door – until they came to the end of the street. They parked in front of a massive white-washed villa with a huge burnished-wood double front door.

"Wowza," Avery said. "This place looks massive."

"It has to be if it's gonna fit all of us, plus it has to have like communal rooms for filming and all that."

"Where do the producers sleep? The cameramen?"

"No clue. I've never done one of these before." Cherylynn laughed, as if to say, Who would possibly go on a dating reality show more than once?

"I have." The beauty next to them reapplied her lip gloss and tucked a loose tendril of hair behind her ear. "The producers and cameramen will also stay on site, or very close, just in case of any drama. They'll have cameras set up in every corner of the house, so remember that too. You're always being watched."

"Even in the bathroom?" Avery gasped.

"Well, you obviously get some privacy there. But not much."

"Just how many reality shows have you been on?" Cherylynn asked the girl.

"I don't know, probably six or seven? It builds my Instagram followers. I'm an influencer, so I have to stay on top of all the new trends."

"Um…" Avery wasn't sure what to say to that. She'd never considered being a "influencer" a career choice, and had about a gazillion questions as to how one could make money from that. But since the van doors were opening, she changed course. "I'm Avery, by the way."

"I'm Lisette. Girl on the Go."

"Girl on the go where?" Avery tilted her head at Lisette in question.

"That's my Instagram handle."

"Oh, right. Got it. I… huh. I suppose I should get on Instagram one of these days."

For the first time, true emotion ran over Lisette's face as she looked at Avery in shock. The rest of the van had quieted, all turning to look at her, while Roman stood by the door, a weird little smirk on his face as he measured her.

"You're. Not. On. Instagram?" Lisette choked out. She might as well have said something like, 'You murdered your father?'

The rest of the van all shook their head sadly at Avery as they piled out of the car; Avery just looked to Cherylynn, who shrugged. Clambering over the seats, Avery allowed Roman to help her from the van.

"I think you just broke all their brains," Roman whispered and Avery laughed at him, surprised at his wit.

"I didn't realize it was a bad thing."

"It's not. At least to the likes of me. For them? It might as well be a punishable offense. Good luck,"

Roman said, sliding the van door closed and nodding to where the women shot Avery suspicious glances.

"I mean… what am I going to take pictures of? My gym routine every day? My houseplants?" Avery grumbled to Cherylynn, who chuckled softly under her breath.

"It's okay. Not everyone has to be on social media. I think it's just that a lot of these women come on shows like this to build their followers and their social currency. It isn't just a game to them – it's a platform to launch their brands and all that."

"Ah, I suppose that makes some sense. I still can't understand why anyone would do this, but at the very least, if they're brand-building that means there's some sort of concentrated effort toward benefiting from this experience."

"If you can't understand why anyone would do this, why are you here?" Roman asked from behind Avery's shoulder, making her jump.

"Um, on a dare?" Avery said, cringing that she'd essentially called his show worthless.

"What was the dare?"

"To break me out of my comfort zone."

"What's your comfort zone?" Roman asked, and Avery felt her back go up. She wished she could see his eyes behind the mirrored sunglasses he wore.

"None of your business," Avery bit out, causing Roman to smile.

"But it is my business. I'm filming you and we're all

about making people vulnerable so we see who they truly are at their core."

"Cool. Great." Avery huffed out a breath and turned away from him, wondering why this man put her on edge so much. It was like he wanted to peel all her carefully built layers away.

"You still didn't answer the question," Roman said, his voice soft at her ear.

She felt a little shiver run down her neck at his nearness. "I'm not obligated to answer all your questions."

"You kind of are. You agreed to it during filming, especially when we do our confessionals and one-on-one interviews."

"Is this a confessional? Right now? Doesn't seem that way to me." Avery spun around, hands on her hips as she went toe-to-toe with him. Finding her eyes at his chest, she tilted her head way up until she could glare at his sunglasses.

"Fair enough. I'll add it to my notes for our interviews." Roman grinned at her, coolly unflappable, and Avery felt a perverse need to punch him in the gut. Instead, she turned away from him, rolling her eyes at a grinning Cherylynn. Roman moved past them to bring the group together, the women quieting down as he raised his arms above his head to get everyone's attention.

"I don't like him," Avery decided.

"Don't get on his bad side. Remember – he can edit you any way he wants."

"Shit," Avery groaned, belatedly realizing that the cameras had just filmed all of that.

"It'll be okay. Just don't let your temper get the better of you and you'll be fine. Be you, first and foremost. Don't act for the cameras. At the end of the day, you have to live with yourself and your behavior."

"That's sound advice."

"Take it from me, girl. Daddy was a preacher."

"Well, then, amen to that."

CHAPTER 4

"*W*elcome to *Swept Away*, ladies," Roman said, and all the women – except Avery – cheered. "This is Villa Azul, and will be our home base for filming, hanging out, and relaxing. Your bachelor will not stay here with you, but will be close by."

The women booed at that.

"I know, I know," Roman said, shrugging his shoulders. "But that's the way of things. We've lucked out with this villa that instead of having four to a room, there'll be two to a room, and each room has its own bathroom. Which, as you are aware if you know anything about reality shows, is a positive luxury."

More cheers from the women.

Lisette looked so relieved that Avery thought the woman might faint in gratitude.

"Roomie?" Cherylynn asked.

"Please," Avery breathed.

"On it," Cherylynn said.

Avery looked at her in confusion until she realized that all the women were poised to run.

"Wait... what?" Avery said, and then almost jumped when the women took off running into the villa, Cherylynn included, all squealing and shrieking as they raced up the stairs. Shouts echoed through the open-air villa as people found their rooms, the cameramen following closely to record any potential drama.

"You sleeping outside?" Roman asked, crossing his arms over his chest as he studied her.

"No way. I just... I wasn't expecting everyone to take off running. There were no instructions on how to pick a room," Avery said, hefting her tote bag on her shoulder and moving toward the villa.

"It's kind of a free-for-all. It appears that women don't follow instructions well."

At that, Avery stopped and turned, glaring over her shoulder at Roman.

"That's incredibly rude. You're painting all women with a wide brush stroke."

"I'm sorry." Roman pinched his nose and sighed. "You're absolutely right. That was an asshole thing to say and I do try not to be an asshole. I just find that, sometimes on these shows, no matter how carefully you spell things out, nobody follows the instructions anyway."

"I can understand that. But that could be due to the intelligence or personalities of your candidates, not their gender."

"That's fair, and again, I apologize. I'll work on filtering myself better."

"That would be appreciated. This is already stressful enough without the peanut gallery making rude comments. Isn't your job to make us feel more comfortable and open up?" Avery had no idea why she was unloading on this man, but all her nervous energy was building up to make her want to take someone's head off. And Roman had just provided her with the perfect excuse.

"At ease, solider. You're absolutely right, and I'm in the wrong." Roman held up his hands in defense, a practiced smile on his face, and Avery wondered just how many women he'd used that on.

"Good. Just remember that," she huffed, turning and stomping inside.

Cherylynn leaned over a railing on the second floor and called to her. "Avery! Up here! I got us a room."

"Coming," Avery said, and veered toward the staircase, barely glancing at the massive open-air main floor. Her mind whirled with a million thoughts and impressions, and a part of her wished she had five minutes to just pull out her notebook and write everything down so she could assess how she felt about all of this... this *whatever* she'd signed on for.

The staircase was one of those free-floating open-air ones, and Avery immediately lifted her eyes from where she could see the floor below her between the steps. She grasped the railing tightly. Why would anyone design a staircase this way? Anyone could slip and have their leg go right through – wouldn't that be painful? Not to mention if there was alcohol involved. Avery shuddered at the thought, and then wondered if that was one of the reasons the producers had picked such a place. She supposed a tumble on the stairs would make for good television, if you were into the whole slapstick comedy thing. Breathing a small sigh of relief when she reached the upstairs hallway, Avery brushed past women racing up and down the hallway, poking their heads into various rooms and emitting all kind of shrieks and squeals that had Avery wishing for her noise-cancelling head-phones. Turning her head from the cameraman, she ducked into the room she'd seen Cherylynn disappear into.

"Well, this is nicer than I was expecting." Avery stopped and scanned the room. Two single beds with bright blue linens were separated by a little sitting area with two low-slung chairs and a table. Narrow French doors led to a balcony where Avery could just glimpse the sea beyond. A door in the corner led to what Avery presumed was the bathroom. She didn't particularly care what the bathroom looked like, so long as she could pee in peace without a cameraman kneeling in front of her goods.

"Not bad, right? Plus we have an ocean view balcony. Just remember –" Cherylynn nodded up to the corners of the room, and Avery followed the direction of her gesture to see cameras posted in two separate corners of the lofted ceiling.

"Weird," Avery breathed, tossing her bag onto her bed. Reaching into her purse, she texted Ruby.

I'm here. I'm safe. And I'm imagining all the ways I'll torture you. I think I'll start with shaving your head.

Don't be so dramatic. It'll be great. Promise. How are the other women?

Self-involved. Influencers. Except for my roomie. She's cool.

See? Making friends already.

I don't need more friends. I need to not be on a reality show. They film you while you sleep. Do you know how creepy that is?

Well, just pull the covers up.

I hate you.

Love you too. Go get 'em, tiger. Win that money and pay off the bills! You'll thank me for this. I have a good feeling about it all.

I don't.

Give it a chance.

I gotta go, they're calling us and telling us to bring our phones.

I bet they take them from you.

What!

Standard operating procedure on a reality show. If I don't hear from you, I'll assume that's what happened.

What if I die swimming in the ocean? You'll think I'm just chilling here having fun and have no clue.

I'm sure they'll contact family if there's an emergency. Stop fussing so much. These shows don't want that kind of liability. They'll keep you safe.

I think they want to see us get hurt. There's an open-air staircase here. You know how I feel about those.

Yes, but despite what you may think, those aren't designed specifically so people hurt themselves.

You don't know that.

Avery.

Ruby.

I love you.

Sigh, fine, me too. But I still kind of hate you.

Byeeeee. Have fun!!

"Grr," Avery said, wanting to throw her phone. Instead she smiled at Cherylynn. "Sorry, family being annoying."

"I get that. I have six brothers and sisters. They're always up in my business," Cherylynn said, typing just as furiously on her phone. "I suspect they want us to turn our phones in."

"That's just ridiculous. What if someone at home needs to reach us?"

"You should have been given all that information to give to your family," Cherylynn said.

Avery realized that Ruby probably did indeed have that information. "Right, right. I know. I'm just used to having my phone for emergencies and all that."

"Do you handle a lot of emergencies?" Cherylynn asked as they wandered down the hall. Avery noted that many of the girls had changed already, but she hadn't thought to bring her bags into the room yet. Oh well, she thought with a sigh; her plane outfit would have to do.

"More work stuff. Engineers are constantly getting

called on to problem-solve, so we're usually fairly attached to our methods of communication."

"Well, get ready to be unattached." Cherylynn nodded to where the girls were reluctantly handing their phones over to Roman.

"Gah! Do you think I could hide mine?" Avery wondered.

"Nah, the cameras'll find you. They always do. It'll be fine, Avery. Promise."

"You keep saying that."

"Well? No point in taking a pessimistic view of all this. It might be the coolest thing we do in our lives. Or the near future, at least. Might as well embrace it!"

"Yes, Avery, might as well embrace it," Roman smirked at her side. She almost jumped again. The man was like a cat.

"Fine, here's my phone," Avery said, shutting down her phone and handing it to him. He slid it into a bag marked with Ruby's name on it, then put Cherylynn's into her assigned bag as well.

"Don't worry. If there's anything serious at any time – on your end or at home – you have the right to use your phone. Just tell me and I'll get you a phone, or I'll find you immediately if you're needed. We take the phones away for better television, but we want you to know that you can always be reached or use a phone if you really need to. This isn't a prison."

"That's fair. Thanks, Roman." Cherylynn beamed at him.

He nodded. "Ready for the briefing on the rules?"

"I guess…" Avery said, with one last glance at the bag that held her phone.

"A little more enthusiasm?"

"Yay! Do you have a notebook so I can take notes? I usually use my Notes app on my phone," Avery said.

Roman just leveled a stare at her. Realizing that he wasn't wearing his sunglasses, Avery was startled to see his eyes were a cool grey color, standing out in his face like a port in a storm. The steadiness she saw there calmed her, and she found herself smiling at him, realizing she was being ridiculous.

"As you seem to have a modicum of intelligence, I don't suspect you'll need to take notes," Roman assured Avery.

"It's not too hard, Avery. They'll explain the rules before each challenge too." Cherylynn tugged her over to a white couch. The main floor was massive, with an entire wall of glass doors that were slid open to encourage the sea breezes. Beyond the doors a wide deck wrapped the house, and the sea was only steps away down a sandy beach. Inside, couches and armchairs were scattered around the room to create various conversation areas. A sprawling dining room table in rough-hewn wood claimed one corner of the room, while a massive kitchen island dominated the other, and the kitchen boasted two sinks, two stoves, and two double-door refrigerators. Huge bamboo fans wafted the air lazily above them, and the décor was done in neutrals – greys, whites, and natural wood tones. Nothing to really distract the eye from the brilliant blue of the water just outside the villa.

"This is a beautiful spot. I can't believe we're right on the water."

"See? There you go. Looking at the good. Okay, shhh, they're fixin' to make an announcement."

"As you all know, you've signed up for a reality show called *Swept Away*," Roman began, standing in front of the doors and smiling at them all. Avery couldn't tell how she knew he was putting on a fake smile; perhaps it was the way it didn't light up the rest of his face. "I'm Roman Michellen and I'm the producer of this show. A little bit about me and my role in this production – I've filmed several reality shows, some of which you may have heard of."

Roman listed off a roster of shows that had the women in the group nodding, while Avery was left trying to remember which of the shows on his list were ones that her sister had forced her to watch.

"However, my true love lies in directing and producing travel and nature documentaries. I've also had a lot of success in that area, and once the shooting here is wrapped, I'll be leaving this show to head to Africa to follow an elephant preserve. That being said, I'm still happy to be here because Siren Island is beautiful, and I hope each and every one of you will take some time to embrace the natural elements and rhythms this stunning island has to offer you."

One girl, so heavily made up that Avery wondered how she got anything done every day if she had to apply all that crud to her face, wrinkled her nose in disgust at the word 'nature.' Avery was beginning to see why certain elements of this show might actually be entertaining.

"For the first day, we'll just get you used to having cameras around. There will be no challenges or anything like that. For now, just unpack, chill, go to the beach, do whatever you'd do on a normal day of vacation. Tonight, you'll finally get to meet your bachelor at the opening ceremony, as well as some local friends and mentors who will assist you on your challenges."

A cheer rose from the crowd at the mention of the elusive bachelor. Avery imagined everyone was dying to know just whom they were supposed to woo. A part of her hoped it would be a nice guy, but she supposed that didn't make for good television.

"A few notes on the rules. Don't look at or speak directly to the cameras. For the most part, we want you to forget about the cameramen altogether and let them fade into the background. Another rule – no swimming in the ocean at night. Typically, I'd be fine with it, but knowing how these parties can get at night, I don't want anyone drinking and going in the dark water. It'll be tough to spot you, and safety comes first."

No worries on that front, Avery thought. Her stomach churned at the thought.

"Next up, we'll be basing our challenges on themes that are important in a successful relationship. You won't know until after your challenge which theme you're competing on, but I suggest you write down what you think makes for a strong relationship and try to keep those characteristics in mind as you compete during a challenge. Your score will be revealed after the challenge. At any time, the bachelor can vote someone off. For the first two challenges, the group can vote to bring someone back as well. After that, points and bachelor's choice will determine the winner. Remember, this is about competing in challenges that will help you grow as a person, as well as building a foundation with a man who will hopefully be a strong future partner for you."

"And the prize?" Lisette asked, looking stunning in a slinky silver dress.

"The prize is $100,000 per person to the couple, but you must both choose each other."

"Why does he win money if he doesn't do the challenges?" Cherylynn wondered out loud, then clapped a hand over her mouth.

"He'll be doing the challenges with you too, so I guess the reward is he gets money too."

"Weird," Avery said, but softly. Her mind was whirling with the rules. Basically, she had to complete a bunch of challenges, *and* make this dude fall for her, before she could pay off her bills. A headache began to bloom as she took in her competition and realized that all the other women had begun to do the same. The energy of the room had shifted from fun to calculating.

"Whoa, Nellie. Game on," Cherylynn whispered.

CHAPTER 5

"I still don't understand why the prize is so high," Avery said to Cherylynn. They were stretched out beneath an umbrella by the pool they'd discovered once the meeting had disbanded and everyone was allowed to explore. Avery felt overdressed in her simple black tank suit, compared to the thin scraps of nylon that covered the other women who wandered casually around the deck, striking poses and pretending like the cameras weren't following their every move. In contrast, Avery had on a wide-brimmed straw hat and big sunglasses, and had generously covered her milky white skin in a reef-safe sunscreen. Even though she had zero inclination to head into the ocean anytime soon, she still did her best to pay attention to the environment. Next to her on the table was her latest read, a study on global warming, and her banged-up reusable water bottle. On the lounge to her right, Cherylynn paged through a celebrity gossip magazine, looking sassy in her sparkly blue bikini, a poster girl for the All-American Girl Next Door.

"I think because it will entice people to push harder during the challenges," Cherylynn said. "I mean, if everyone was just trying to win the guy's love with nothing more on the line, why would they fight as hard? I don't think most of us actually expect to find true love here."

"I guess that makes sense. People will often fight more for money than for love."

"Maybe at first. Once attachments form, then they fight for love."

"Ahh, so the money is like an enticement to get people to give it their all from the beginning."

"Basically – at least that's how it reads to me."

"I wish I had her confidence," Avery said, nodding to where Lisette preened in a tiny scrap of red bikini, which left essentially all of her bum revealed and a generous portion of her cleavage on display.

"She's just flaunting it," Cherylynn decided.

"She's got it. She can flaunt it. I would love to be half as comfortable in my skin as she is." Avery honestly admired the ease with which Lisette navigated the pool area, even though she was all but naked.

"Why wouldn't you be? You've got a fantastic body. Good muscle tone. Good curves. Healthy head of hair."

Avery snorted. "You sound like you're evaluating a horse to buy."

"Sorry, that's the rancher's daughter in me." Cherylynn shrugged.

"I thought you said your dad was a preacher."

"He's that too. Small-town Texas. Lots of roles to play."

"Ladies," Roman said, stopping in front of them. His mirrored sunglasses were back on, and Avery found she preferred that to looking into his eyes. She felt more in control when he was behind a protective shield.

"Hello." Cherylynn beamed up at him.

"That's a good book," Roman said, nodding to Avery's book. "Have you read it or is it just for show?"

Avery sighed and shook her head at him sadly.

"Didn't we discuss your attitude already?"

Roman grimaced and then shrugged, a sheepish smile tugging across his handsome face.

"Sorry. Again. I'm obviously a work in progress. I just don't see a lot of these types of books at gatherings like this one."

"Just because you don't see it doesn't mean they aren't there," Avery said. "For all you know, Lisette may have studied microbiology." They all turned to study Lisette as she arched her back and stuck out her breasts for the camera.

"She's a makeup artist from Chicago," Roman smiled.

"You still don't know what she reads for pleasure. Maybe she loves being creative with makeup but secretly wishes to be a scientist."

"Maybe. I'll ask her in one of our confessional interviews," Roman promised.

"Good. You should. People can surprise you."

"Speaking of, the party starts in an hour or so. Plan for your first interviews this evening. We'll formally begin taping tonight."

"We'll be ready," Cherylynn promised as he walked away. Then she all but pounced on Avery.

"What was that about?"

"What?"

"That." Cherylynn nodded to Roman.

"What?"

"*That*! Don't be ridiculous. Clearly there's tension between you two."

"Um, the only tension is that he's kind of an asshole. Which he, himself, admitted after he made some rude comments earlier today."

"Sure, he clearly has a bias on some things, but I don't think he's an asshole. I mean, he makes documentaries about saving nature and stuff. That doesn't sound like an asshole to me."

"He still produces reality television."

"Duh, because it makes a shit-ton more money than producing documentaries. He probably does this to foot the bills while he traipses through the bush trying to save baby elephants." Cherylynn sighed and fanned herself. "I'm liking him more and more."

"Don't romanticize him," Avery said with a laugh and shook her head at Cherylynn.

"Why not? Isn't that what this is all about?"

"Romance? Maybe, maybe not. I'm doing my best to withhold judgment on all of this."

"Taking it all in?"

"Pretty much."

"How very engineer of you," Cherylynn said, and then rolled to look at Avery. "But in all seriousness though, be careful."

"Of Roman? Why? I'm not interested in him."

"Not Roman. Of this show. See, you're being nice and giving everyone the benefit of the doubt. But these women won't do that for you. You have no idea what's driving them to be on this show or what the stakes are. Remember, nobody's your friend here."

"Not even you?" Avery tilted her head at Cherylynn.

"I mean… yes, of course me, but also, who knows? What if I blurt out your secrets under the duress of a challenge or something? I'm not the best at keeping secrets anyway."

"Okay, duly noted. I won't share what I don't want on television. How about that?"

"That's fair. I don't want to *not* be your friend. I just worry… competition makes people do ugly things," Cherylynn said, biting her lower lip.

"Well, let's do our best to hold our heads up high and live with our behavior. Deal?"

"Deal. Now let's go make ourselves beautiful. Opening ceremony will be a showstopper."

Avery was a little bummed that she hadn't gotten to read even a chapter of her book, but she suspected reading wouldn't be high on the list of priorities during her stay here. She smiled and nodded at all the women she passed, continuing to marvel at their beauty, and followed Cherylynn to their room where they immediately dove into their half-unpacked bags.

"Is this an entire bag of survival gear?" Cherylynn peered into Avery's duffel.

"Yup. This is the one I packed. The other one was –" Avery caught herself. "...packed by my best friend, who is the fashionista. I even have outfit instructions."

"Um, that's amazing. I wish I had that." Cherylynn pulled out a slinky green silk dress from a hanging bag. "I was thinking this for tonight."

"It's stunning. You absolutely should. Let me just, ah, consult my notes." Avery felt her cheeks heat as she paged through the little notebook until she found the image her sister had labeled for opening ceremony. "Okay, it looks like this... and this... and I have instructions on jewelry too." She pulled out a pink slip dress the color of sand-washed shells, its neckline sparkling with intricate beading, then put it aside to find the nude strappy wedges to go with it.

As a redhead, she typically avoided wearing pinks and reds. Digging in her jewelry case, Avery found the turquoise statement earrings Ruby had assigned to go with the dress. What had she been thinking? It was a weird color combination, and she was certain she'd look ridiculous in it.

"Oh, that's fabulous," Cherylynn breathed, and Avery turned to her in shock.

"It is?"

"It is. That color will look amazing on you. Do you

want to shower first or second? I can help you with your hair."

"Great, because the only thing I know about my hair is letting it do its monster-curl thing or putting it in a messy bun."

"Both of which work for you. So hop to it." Cherylynn pointed and Avery dutifully made her way to the bathroom. Taking the quickest shower she could, Avery let the tension from a long day of travel ease from her shoulders. It's going to be okay, she reminded herself. Stepping outside her comfort zone wasn't meant to be, well, comfortable.

A short while later, Avery found herself following Cherylynn through the main room and down to the beach where cushions and benches had been arranged in a half-circle around a fire pit. The sun, almost kissing the horizon, sent rays of pure gold across the calm water.

"Well, everyone's outdone themselves," Cherylynn decided, scanning the group of beautiful women who had turned out in their best fashion. For once, Avery was glad she had let Ruby take control when it came to her wardrobe, because she didn't feel out of place. If anything, after standing in front of the mirror and seeing what her sister had pulled together, Avery felt more confident than usual. The pink dress did wonders for her skin and made her auburn curls pop. The turquoise earrings stood out against her hair. Cherylynn had braided one side of her hair and left the rest to tumble in a wild mess over her shoulders. She felt chic, a little extravagant, and like maybe she could actually be a contender in this game.

"Champagne?" A waiter smiled at them with a tray in his hands.

"No thanks," Avery said, remembering what Roman had said about alcohol and good television. The waiter just stood there patiently until she relented and took a glass.

"Even if you don't drink it, I think they want us all to hold it for the photos and video," Cherylynn said.

"Fine, I'll dump mine in the sand after."

"Don't waste good champagne! I'll drink it."

They quickly found a seat on one of the benches as a man stepped forward and lit the fire. The bugs were already out, as they were wont to be at any sunset on any island ever, and Avery was grateful for the bug repellent she'd applied liberally before they'd left the room. Cherylynn had just rolled her eyes, but now, watching the women swat at mosquitos and sand flies, Avery was pleased with her forethought.

"Don't sit there looking all smug like the cat who ate the canary," Cherylynn whispered as she swatted another mosquito.

"Was I? Hmmm, I was just enjoying this lovely night."

"Uh-huh. The fire will chase them away."

"Sure thing. Until then…" Despite not wanting to drink, Avery took a small sip of her glass and smiled.

"See? Smug."

"Shhh," Avery said, motioning to where two men

approached, both equally handsome in their own ways. She wondered which one was their bachelor. Unless there were maybe two?

"Good evening, ladies." The first man, with short dark hair and tanned skin, smiled at them. "I'm Jack Lyndon and I'll be your host for the show. Which means, as I'm sure you can figure out, that this hand-some man next to me is your bachelor, Beckett Smith."

Avery raised her eyebrows as Beckett – blond, tanned, and rippling with muscles – executed a casual backflip on the sand before gracing all the ladies with a million-dollar smile. Over half the women squealed and clapped their hands. Avery rolled her eyes.

"Oh boy, we've got a live one, don't we?" Chery-lynn murmured.

Avery just took another sip of her champagne. She was going to need it.

CHAPTER 6

*R*oman watched as Beckett preened for the ladies, nodding to his cameramen to circle around and get reaction shots to his little display of foolishness.

He'd hated Beckett on sight.

Which wasn't entirely fair of him, Roman thought as he stood in the shadows and watched the women's reaction to Beckett's introduction. He'd picked the guy, after all. Roman knew what made for good television, and a peacock like Beckett would have the viewers divided. Which meant they would come back episode after episode, half of them wanting Beckett to fail, the other half hoping he would find love. All in all, factoring in what he'd sized up from the contestants and the island itself, this would make for engrossing reality television.

Which made Roman even more annoyed at himself. This was not what he'd gone to school for, this was not his passion – and yet the money had been too good to turn down. He had turned out to have a knack for producing reality shows that hooked people, and now he was highly sought after in the genre. Unfortunately, his heart was elsewhere, and he was doing his best to support his passion while taking on projects like these. It was about balance, he reminded himself; not everyone had the luxury of only doing what they were passionate about for a living. At the very least, these reality shows funded his lifestyle such that he could afford to pay his crew what they deserved for following him into the wilds of whatever country he set his sights on. It was important to him to pay all of his people a fair wage, which was why he was highly respected in the industry.

And yet, here he was, Roman thought, promising himself this would be the last show like this he did. His eyes slid to where Avery sat, looking like a rose waiting to be plucked, her dress shimmering in the flames. He smiled when he caught her eyeroll at Beckett's antics. She wouldn't make it long on the show with that attitude, but damn, he liked her for it.

"She's lovely, no?"

"Damn, Irma. You scared me half to death," Roman said, keeping his voice low as he turned to the woman at his side.

"For a man who traipses the bush in search of lions, you should be more attuned to a person's approach."

"Fair enough. If you marry me and run away with me, you could stalk lions in the bush too, you know," Roman said, smiling at Irma. He was only half-joking, having been utterly entranced with Irma since the day he'd Skyped with her several months ago. With luscious grey hair, eyes that saw everything, and a curvy body, Irma was every man's dream at any age. She was beauty, life, wisdom, and sensuality all packed into one. For once in his life, he wished he was an artist – he could just envision painting Irma as she emerged from the sea, a storm raging around her.

"I've told you before, this island is my home. I'd offer my daughters for you to date, but they have minds of their own, as you well know," Irma laughed, sliding her arm through Roman's as she studied the group.

"Your daughters are just as beautiful as you, but I find them both terrifying."

"And I'm not?" Irma asked, delighted with him.

"You are. But not like they are. I pity the man who tries to win them over. Jolie will eat them alive, while Mirra will sweetly poison them."

"Then I've taught them well," Irma decided.

"The cameras are going to love you all. I'm even more interested to see how the women respond to you. I suspect many will be threatened."

"By me? Nonsense. By my girls – well, that's not a surprise. I've raised two beautiful women."

"I'd say you're all more than beautiful. It's not just what you look like, but how your souls shine through. The three of you are luminous."

"I like you, Roman," Irma said, squeezing his arm. "You are welcome at my table any day."

"I plan to take you up on that."

"Now, tell me about the girl you were mooning over."

"That would be you, Irma," Roman said, neatly deflecting the question.

"Ah, you're good for my ego, young one," Irma laughed, but nodded to Avery. "Her. The knockout redhead in the pink dress. You like her."

"I… I don't not like her. She intrigues me, I'll admit. She seems oddly baffled by this whole thing. Says she came here on a dare. She was reading a non-fiction book on the climate crisis at the pool today. I find her a breath of fresh air among everyone else, I guess."

"Her energy is good. Wounded, a bit, from something. You'll help her bloom," Irma decided. Then, releasing Roman's hand, she began making her way toward Jack, who was motioning to her.

"Wait… no, I won't…" Roman started to say, and then clamped his mouth shut, because cameras were rolling.

"Gotta love our mother. She sure likes to drop a bomb, no?" Jolie said, coming to stand on one side of Roman. Her dark hair curled wildly around her shoulders and she'd poured her curvy body into a sequined teal minidress, and Roman imagined every man in America sitting up to beg.

"You let him be, Jolie. He's still figuring this all out," Mirra said. Roman glanced to his other side to see Mirra, looking like an ethereal angel in a slim column of white, her blond hair flowing in two loose braids over her shoulder. It was like being bookended by fire and water, and Roman couldn't decide which was more enticing.

"Thanks, ladies. Your turn to head on up. Go make those women jealous," Roman said, nodding to the front of the circle.

"I thought you wanted us to mentor them," Mirra pouted.

"You will. But they'll still be jealous of you. That's okay. You're both amazing. Just be you and the rest will shine through."

He had stumbled upon the Laughing Mermaid guest-house when he was scouting locations for this show. When he'd seen pictures of the owners, he immediately got on a video call with them to see if they'd be interested in the show. Not only would they play an integral part in mentoring and guiding this group of women on their journey here, but they were also the perfect foils for weeding out the jealous ones in the bunch. He'd be able to size up who would make for good television, and who would actually be a match for Beckett, simply by watching how the group of women responded to the knockouts who lived at the Laughing Mermaid.

Judging by the way Beckett's tongue all but fell out of his mouth when the sisters approached, Roman knew he'd chosen well. Now, he just had to sit back and watch the show.

And stay away from Avery, Roman chided himself. Poking at her was going to get in the way of him producing great television. Despite his misgivings about taking on this project, he prided himself on doing his job well. He'd chosen to take this job, and he would produce the hell out of this show.

No matter what.

CHAPTER 7

"*B*eckett, why don't you tell us a little bit about yourself," Jack said, directing the attention to Beckett. Avery disliked him immediately and wondered just how long she'd be able to even keep up her pretense in this game.

"Laaaadies," Beckett said, smiling at the crowd of beautiful women around him, seeming as pleased as could be. And how could he not be? He had sixteen stunning women dying to meet him. "I'm Beckett, I run a surf camp in California, and I oversee a non-profit that helps children with disabilities spend time in the water."

"Um," Cherylynn said, turning to look at Avery.

"I was not expecting that," Avery admitted.

The group of women all cooed in approval and Beckett nodded enthusiastically, basking in their praise.

"I feel like he just does a job like that to get women," Avery said.

"Could be. Either way, the ovaries of every woman here just sat up and cheered."

Avery took another sip of her champagne to stop herself from snorting in laughter.

"He knows it, too. See?" Avery whispered as she watched Beckett lapping up the praise from the women.

"Girl, I've got eyes, don't I?" Cherylynn said. "That being said, he's hot."

"If you're into the blond surfer boys."

"Who isn't?"

"I don't know. Not me. I like dark, quiet, brooding," Avery mused. Her last boyfriend, Mr. Outdoors himself, had been a blond surfer type. Maybe she had a bit of post-traumatic stress from her accident, she realized, given that she hadn't dated a blond guy since.

"Like Roman," Cherylynn whispered.

"Like who? What? No, not Roman," Avery griped. "Stop with that. He's not my type."

"Mmmhmm."

"Ladies, we'd like to introduce another integral part of our show this season – Irma, who will mentor you on your way, and her two daughters, Jolie and Mirra. All three live here and run the Laughing Mermaid guesthouse. They'll be a resource to you and help you during... times of turbulence, let's just say, as we go through these challenges together."

"Oh my god." Cherylynn clutched Avery's hand as three of the most stunning women Avery had ever seen in her life stepped into the light. Judging from the silence that greeted them, everyone else was equally bowled over by their beauty.

Including Beckett, who had turned and was eyeing Jolie like a snack he wanted to taste.

Avery was transfixed by Irma. While her age was indeterminate, she was beautiful in an ageless way. She wore not a drop of makeup, her flowing dress the color of sunset, with long crystal necklaces adding just the touch of embellishment she needed. Irma was an every-woman, and Avery wouldn't have been surprised if she'd been birthed straight from the sea.

Amused at her fanciful thoughts, Avery glanced down to see her champagne glass was empty. That explained that, she thought, and gently put the glass down in the sand.

"Welcome to our little island," Irma said. "It's a pure joy to be in the presence of such beauty. We look forward to helping you on your journey. Remember, we are here as resources to you, whether it's to talk something out or to offer assistance on a challenge. Don't be afraid to come to us, as our door is always open."

The women all clapped politely, clearly unsure how to proceed in the face of such magnificence. Beckett had yet to turn back from eyeing Jolie and give his attention to the group of women, and Avery saw more than one woman frown.

"Uh-oh. Trouble in paradise," she murmured.

"Isn't it? I need to ask that Mirra how she gets her hair like that. It's marvelous."

"Looks like we'll have a chance, too. Time to

mingle," Avery said, after Jack announced food, music, and dancing was on for the rest of the night.

"Let's go. I need to eat something fierce," Chery-lynn said, eying up the buffet table.

"Don't you want to meet your bachelor?"

"Nah. He's busy right now. Give him time."

"I'm going to say hi to the women first. I'll meet you by the food," Avery decided. There was something drawing her to Jolie and Mirra. Maybe it was their obvious bond of sisterhood, something which resonated strongly for Avery.

"Hi, I'm Avery," she said, coming to a stop where the three women stood by themselves. The rest of the group had given these women a wide berth in order to fawn over Beckett.

"We were wondering if anyone was going to come talk to us," Jolie said, tossing her hair over her shoulder. "I'm glad it was you. Love your earrings."

"Thank you. Your dress is killer," Avery said automatically.

Jolie grinned. "I like you already."

"You like anyone who compliments you," Mirra said, nudging Jolie before holding out her hand. "A pleasure to meet you."

"I think all three of you are the most beautiful women I've ever seen," Avery admitted, glad the dark-ness would hide her blush. She felt a rush of warmth go through her when Irma enveloped her in a hug.

"That's very kind of you to say," Irma said, pulling

back but keeping her hands on Avery's shoulders, studying her. "I think you'll do well here."

"Can I be you when I grow up?" Avery asked, and then almost bit her tongue. Irma threw back her head and laughed.

"Get in line," Jolie said, and they all joined in the laughter.

"Why do you say I'll do well here? I honestly don't think I'm cut out for all this," Avery admitted, turning to look at where Beckett swept a girl off her feet and pretended to run away with her.

"I didn't mean the show," Irma said.

"You mean… like *here*? On Siren Island?"

"You'll do well here." Irma didn't bother to elaborate, instead squeezing her shoulder once more as Cherylynn bounced over, a cookie in her hand.

"I'm sorry, y'all, I just had to get some food in my stomach." Cherylynn grinned and the ladies of the Laughing Mermaid beamed right back at her. "Pleased to meet y'all."

"I like you too," Jolie decided.

"You two are the only ones speaking to us," Mirra agreed.

"The rest are too intimidated by you. I just want to know how you got your hair to look like that?" Cherylynn asked and in moments they were deep in discussion about hair products, humidity, and saltwater.

"What brings you to the show, Avery?" Jolie asked. "If this isn't really your thing?"

"It was a dare," Avery said, practicing her lying skills.

"That's a lie. But I think you have your own reasons for doing so, plus you've been really nice to us, so I'll let it pass," Jolie said, idly twirling a lock of her midnight hair around her finger.

"Um…" Avery said, her cheeks tinging with heat once more.

"Jolie. Not everyone has to share their secrets right away. Give her time to open up."

"Thank you, and I'm sorry," Avery admitted. "As a rule, I don't lie. It's just… complicated. Can we go with that? I'd like to have friends here and I think you could be them. I don't want to go into that based on mistrust, but I can't tell you my reasons for being here – not yet."

"That's fair. I'd like to be your friend as well," Jolie decided. "Especially if I can borrow those earrings sometime."

"Sold," Avery said, and Jolie took her hand, shaking on it.

If only Avery could understand why it felt like a current of electricity ran through her palm at her touch. Meeting her eyes, she found Jolie studying her, as if waiting for her to say something more.

Instead, Roman chose that moment to appear at her shoulder.

"Interview time, Avery."

"Wait, what? I thought tonight was relaxing and getting to know each other."

"I mentioned earlier tonight would also included

interviews as we're taping. Which means it's your turn. Let's go."

"Fine," Avery bit out and waved a little goodbye to the ladies.

This was going to be a disaster.

CHAPTER 8

"**Why** do I have to be the first for an interview?" Avery grumbled as she followed Roman to a chair sitting across from a cameraman.

"Who said you were the first?"

"It feels like I am."

"You're not."

"Fine, but still. Can't I get some food? Work up to this?"

"No, you're doing your interview now."

"How many of these will I have to do?"

"How long do you plan to be on the show?"

"Are these really necessary?"

"Avery!" Roman's tone was sharp. "Seriously, have you ever seen a reality show? They always interview people separately from the filming. It provides backstory. It gives narration. It helps the viewers get to know the people on the show better.

It's just part of what we do. I'm not punishing you."

"Fine, fine, sorry. I'm cranky. I didn't eat much today," Avery said, settling into the chair and shooting a pouty look at the cameraman.

"I totally understand. I get hangry all the time," the cameraman said, nodding in agreement.

Avery beamed at him. "See?"

"You may eat. In ten minutes. Let's just get through this," Roman snapped.

Avery sighed. "Fine. What do you want me to say?"

"Tell me who you are."

"Hi, I'm Avery Deluca. I'm twenty-seven years old, I live in Des Moines, and I'm a environmental engineer with a focus on building sustainable and ecologically friendly infrastructures."

"I was not expecting that," Roman said, surprise crossing his handsome face.

"Why? Because I'm a woman?"

"No, I was just surprised at the specific focus of your career." Roman shifted in his seat.

"So what did you think I did?"

"Trust fund baby?" Roman shrugged.

"No, Roman. I work for a living. Very hard, mind you. And I'm proud of what I do."

"As you should be. I just wasn't expecting it, is all."

Avery sat silently and waited, refusing to give out any other details of her life while Roman paged through his questions.

"Avery, are you religious?"

"Nope."

"Why not?"

"Because I don't believe there is any one way to practice spirituality."

"So you're spiritual?"

"I suppose."

"What led you to believe in the spiritual nature of this world?"

Avery just looked at him as a vivid memory of being in a coma flashed through her mind.

"I think there are too many instances of unexplainable 'otherworldly' type things to dismiss the existence of another plane of the universe. However, I don't like joining groups and I don't think there's any one particular religion that has it right or wrong. I think most people are searching. I do think there is something more out there; I just don't need the rules of a religion to lead me to those answers. Some people do – they enjoy the comfort and framework of a religion to practice their faith within. I'm just not one of them."

"Very pragmatic of you. And yet, not, if you do believe in another plane of existence."

"I suppose."

"Do you believe in soulmates?"

"I haven't thought about it much."

"So… yes? No?"

"I guess there could be someone meant for you. How do you define a soulmate?" Avery demanded, fed up with his line of questioning.

"I define it as someone recognizing intrinsically that another person is meant for them."

"But how can you be meant for someone else? Aren't you meant to follow a path true to yourself? Your needs? Your beliefs? Saying you are 'meant for someone else' implies ownership, doesn't it? I don't want someone to own me," Avery said, batting the idea away with a wave of her hand.

"But wouldn't your soulmate know that about you, then? And give you freedom to be you?"

"But that still implies that things are predestined. Do you believe in destiny or fate?" Avery studied Roman. She barely noticed the camera guys smiling at them.

"Can't I believe in both?" Roman parried.

"That's evading the question. Not all soulmates are fated to meet. So what happens then? They wander, forever looking for their partner? They chose the wrong path and missed their chance?" Avery argued.

"Maybe, maybe not. Perhaps we have several soulmates," Roman said, crossing his arms over his chest.

"Well, let me know when you meet yours, because I'm dying to know how fate led you to them." For some reason, Avery was getting increasingly angry. As an engineer, she didn't leave things to chance. For Roman to make it seem like everyone was one missed connection away from finding their soulmate was preposterous. "Interview over."

Without looking back, Avery stood and strode away, her eyes on the buffet table even though she no longer felt hungry. She knew if she didn't eat soon, she'd probably rip someone's head off.

"Hi, I'm Beckett." The bachelor stopped in front of her and offered his hand. Avery quenched down the urge to brush past him and instead gave him a tight smile.

"Hi, I'm Avery. And I'm absolutely famished. Excuse me while I grab some food. I'll catch up with you after."

Avery didn't wait for his answer, nor did she see him turn and smile approvingly after her.

All she wanted was food, a good book, and her bed.

CHAPTER 9

*I*t didn't look like she would get to her book anytime soon, Avery thought as she crammed another bite of rice in her mouth. She wasn't sure why she was just so annoyed with Roman. The man, by all respects, was just doing what was required by his job. But she certainly hadn't been expecting him to jump right into deep questions – shouldn't he have been asking her what her hobbies were or where her favorite travel destination was?

Perhaps it was just the reminder of her accident that had caused her to get her back up. Avery took another bite from her delicious plate of mixed grill, veggies, and rice, and stared out past the bonfire toward the water. Most of the women were hovering around Beckett anyway or trying to pose for the cameras, both of which held zero interest for Avery. Instead, despite how much she tried to shove it aside, her mind wandered back to the experience she'd had while in a coma.

Most would say it was the drugs. Being medically sedated into a coma certainly could steer people to that conclusion. But she'd never told anyone other than her sister about her experience, so it wasn't like she'd let anyone weigh in on the topic either way. After experiencing… what she'd experienced, Avery had comfortably let the excuse of medical drugs stand in place of what she now knew to be absolutely true.

There were spirits and magic in this world. Not just in the next world, but here and now, actively participating and guiding people about their everyday lives. In all honesty, Avery struggled with the fact that she actually believed this; she tried her best to shove it deep down inside of her and never crack open that particular box to examine too deeply. But she couldn't shake what she knew in her core, and that was… well, that was that.

They had come to her in her coma, her spirit guides. Apparently she had a team of them working on her behalf. They'd shown her the accident, everything that had happened while she'd been blacked out. It was like she'd watched a video of it all from afar. She saw how scared everyone had been, and just how her guides had assisted in little ways to make sure she made it to safety.

One of the guides, a warm female energy, had promised her she'd wake from her coma and that she had big things to do in this world. That love waited for her. And that she should go on with life, promising to take risks and live fearlessly. In doing so, she'd be rewarded with a life rich in adventure and love.

Had Avery followed that advice? Not until now. She'd hidden her head in the proverbial sand as she'd worked through the long recovery after her accident, as well as the lingering trauma that surrounded it. Every once in a while, she felt like she was getting a nudge from the spiritual realm to follow a different path, but thus far she had largely ignored it.

"Is the food not to your taste?"

Avery straightened at Irma's voice at her shoulder. She paused, taking in the sheer force of this woman's presence. There was something about her – equal parts terrifying and soothing – that had Avery's full attention.

"No, it's lovely. I'm just in a mood, I guess." Avery shrugged, pushing the plate away and leaning back in the wicker beach chair she'd commandeered.

"Mind if I join you?"

"Of course not. I'd love to talk to you."

"Thank you." Irma sighed as she adjusted her skirts around her, sinking gracefully into the chair next to Avery and taking a small sip from her drink.

"You must love living here. From what I've seen so far, the island is really beautiful."

"It is. This is home and always has been. I suspect I'd feel like a fish out of water anywhere else."

"I can see the appeal. Beautiful sunsets, easy island pace, beach parties…"

"Well, it's not always a party. There are a lot of inconveniences to living on an island. Break your iPhone? You can't just take it to the Apple store.

Looking for certain ingredients? They may not have arrived at the grocery store this week."

"Ahh, sure, I see."

"But I'll argue that having fewer choices makes for a more peaceful life. One of the things I hear is that people spend their time at all the malls rushing from errand to errand to buy more, more, more. People are just filling their existence with running to the store, buying stuff they don't need, and then going home to flop in front of the television. Here, we don't buy as much of that stuff – well, partly because it's expensive to ship in, but also, we don't need it. Life is more about connecting with other people, or experiencing nature. A day doesn't go by that I'm not in the water at some point. It feels incredible to be connected to nature on such a level."

"I suppose that makes sense. The more choices you have, the more overwhelmed you are. Although don't you miss Starbucks?"

"I've never had Starbucks, so it isn't something I could miss."

"I suppose. Their coffee is overrated anyway. There's a small coffee shop by my work that focuses on sustainable practices, as well as eco-friendly cups and to-go containers. I try to use them as much as possible, because it aligns with my beliefs."

"It's nice to see a shift in people's thoughts lately. I think it's important to honor nature. Especially the sea. Everything leads downstream to the water. Mother Sea is everything to me," Irma said, a wistfulness tinging her voice as she looked out to the waves.

"She terrifies me," Avery admitted before clamping her mouth shut. Why was she giving up all her secrets?

"Is that so? Did something happen to make you feel that way? Or is it just that you're unfamiliar with being around the ocean?"

"I... I had an accident," Avery said, meeting Irma's eyes. "It wasn't in the ocean, but it's made me very fearful of water ever since."

"I hope, for your sake, that you'll be able to move past that. The ocean can heal."

"What do we need to heal?" Beckett stood over them, and Avery leaned back in her chair to look up at him. Cherylynn was right – he was very handsome, even if he wasn't the type of guy she usually went for.

"I'll just leave you two to chat," Irma said, gracefully rising and squeezing Avery's shoulder before melting into the crowd. Beckett dropped into her abandoned seat, his long legs spreading out in front of him, and turned to smile at Avery. She found herself smiling back, and she was keenly aware that the cameras had begun to circle them.

"Nothing, really. Irma was just talking about her love of the ocean and how she finds saltwater to be healing."

"I can agree with that. If you could see these kid's faces once I get them in water – it's like they've had an out-of-body experience. The weightlessness of the water and the freedom of movement it gives them lifts the restrictions they face every day in their wheelchairs or crutches."

"It sounds like you really make a difference in their lives."

"I hope so," Beckett said, dragging a hand casually through his hair and shooting Avery a killer grin. "It feels really great to see their smiles and hear their laughter once they're comfortable in the water."

"How long have you been running this organization?" Avery admired his commitment to his non-profit, yet a part of her wondered if he was one of those guys who loved talking about the good things he did in order to get approval from others. Maybe it was shitty of her to think that of this man she'd just met, but she couldn't help but question his motivations.

"Just over two years now. It was an offshoot of my surf camp. It sort of evolved naturally, but I'm glad to be able to offer it."

"What's a surf camp?"

"What… what do you mean?" Beckett looked at her and gave a little derisive snort, which immediately set Avery on edge. Just because she didn't know what his camp was didn't mean he had to be rude.

"What is it? What do you do? How is it run? Is it a day camp? A week camp? For adults? Children? Do people stay overnight? Do they camp on the beach in tents? Do you train professionals? That's what I mean," Avery said, barely stopping herself from rolling her eyes at him.

"Ah, I see. It's a camp for kids where they can learn to surf. It's a week long or more, depending on how long their parents want to get rid of them." Beckett chuckled, and then winked at another girl who was hovering at the edge of their seating area.

Already annoyed with him and this conversation, Avery abruptly stood. Beckett looked at her in confusion.

"I'm going to get more food," Avery said, even though her plate was half-full. "And it looks like you want to chat with this woman anyway."

"Aw, Avery, are you jealous?"

Avery was so startled by his question that she let out a booming laugh and tossed her hair over her shoulder.

"Not in the slightest, Beckett. Enjoy your evening."

Enjoying the disgruntled look that crossed his face, Avery wandered away from him, looking for a place where she could rid herself of her plate. Normally she would have eaten all her food, but the night's events were making her lose her appetite. Grabbing another glass of champagne, despite what she'd promised herself, she glanced back at the party. The women had gravitated toward the fire and Beckett, beginning to dance in the sand as the alcohol kicked in and the music grew louder. Knowing nobody would miss her, Avery turned the other way, her toes digging into the sand as she walked toward the water.

She wasn't running away, exactly, but she did need a breather.

All she could think was that she'd been an absolute

idiot to come here. Staring out at the water, trying to ignore the ripples of fear that pulsed through her as she looked at the dark waves, Avery saluted the ocean with her glass.

"Here's to breaking out of my comfort zone."

CHAPTER 10

"There's that comfort zone I keep hearing about again," Roman said from behind her.

Avery sighed, turning to glance at him over her shoulder. "I thought you were doing interviews."

"All done. I saw you sneak off toward the water and came to make sure you weren't breaking the rules."

"I'm not a rulebreaker by nature."

"That's too bad. Sometimes rules are meant to be broken."

"When it comes to me and water, you will find me following all the rules ever."

"Something happen there?" Roman came to stand by her, not touching, but she could feel the heat of his nearness.

"Nothing that I care to discuss."

"Listen, I'm sorry if I'm putting you on edge. It's really not my goal to argue with you or make you uncomfortable. In fact, I'm supposed to make you feel *more* comfortable so you're willing to open up to me. I'm not sure why we're butting heads so much, but I hope you know that you can trust me."

"That's a tricky one, though, isn't it?" Avery turned to look at him once more, little flames of the bonfire reflected in his eyes. "Maybe I can trust you, but you still hold power over me. You can edit this show any way you see fit. You can make me look as fragile or bitchy as you'd like. And I couldn't blame you for it, because your first loyalty has to be to producing a great show."

"Is that what you think? Your first loyalty has to be to your job?"

"To your commitments, I'd say, but yes." Avery dug a toe in the sand, turning back to look out at the pale light of the moon dancing across the ripple of water.

"I admire that characteristic. Not everyone follows their ethics so closely." Roman rocked back on his heels, pausing before looking at her once more. "How about this? If you trust me, I promise to portray you fairly on the show. If you go hog-wild and dive over the bonfire and start pulling some girl's hair, well, there isn't much I'll be able to do to conceal that from the cameras. But I promise not to edit you unfairly or intentionally misrepresent the meaning behind your words."

"Do you do that? Is that how you make shows so enticing?"

"I try to stay away from that practice. Mainly

because I think, in these situations, there's already enough drama to keep viewers interested without manufacturing more. Plus, it doesn't really sit well with me to play with people's words to the point where they say the sky is blue and I make it seem like they think the sky is red. It feels just a touch too slimy for me."

"Awww, you do have a heart." Avery tossed him a smile, softening her words.

"I do, at that. But, if it's any reassurance to you, I like you, Avery. I'd like to see you stick around, for many reasons."

"And those would be?" Avery brushed away a strand of hair that blew across her face, and tried to ignore the warmth that rushed through her at his words.

"I think you're smart, you're spunky, and you'll be a palate cleanser after all the other women on the show. For reality television, it's important that people stand out, have a personality, and aren't all the same. And from a personal standpoint, I enjoy my conversations with you, and I think you're interesting to interview. It's a refreshing change of pace."

"So I'm a good contrast for all those beautiful women who are dying to be on television?"

"You're equally if not more beautiful," Roman said, and Avery was stunned to realize she'd been fishing for compliments. What kind of woman did that make her? Sighing, she went to push her glasses up her nose, then remembered they were back in her room next to the note from Ruby reminding her not to wear them on camera.

"I'm sorry, that was ridiculous of me. I think I was fishing for a compliment." Avery laughed at herself. "I guess I do feel very much like a fish out of water here. And when I feel uncomfortable, I have a tendency to pick everything apart or be critical of it."

"I understand; a lot of people do the same. But not all of them would be self-aware enough to acknowledge it and apologize. That's why I like you, Avery."

"Thank you, Roman. I appreciate your kindness. I'll… well, I'll do my best not to make your life hell. And I promise you won't find me going into the water."

"You'll have to tell me about your water thing at some point."

"I don't have to tell you anything that I don't want to tell you. I may have signed papers, but that doesn't mean I owe the viewers anything I don't want to share."

"Do your best to remember that. Viewers will think they know you and everything about you. Reporters will dig. If there's something you don't want found out, I suggest you never reference it here – ever."

"It's not that serious," Avery sighed, then looked over her shoulder as Jolie and Mirra approached. "Hi ladies."

"Hello, you two. We just came over to bust up your makeout session," Jolie said, flipping her wild curls over her shoulder.

"What! We weren't –" Avery sputtered, and Jolie hooted out a laugh, her mini dress shimmering in the moonlight.

"Jolie, stop it. They obviously weren't making out. We could see them from the party," Mirra murmured, patting Avery lightly on the arm.

"More's the pity. There's nothing like stealing away from a party for a good makeout session." Jolie shrugged and then narrowed her eyes. "If no sexy fun times, then what are you two talking about?"

"We're calling a truce," Avery said, smiling as Roman's eyebrows shot up in surprise. He would learn quickly enough that Avery was a straightforward girl.

"Smart. You'll want him on your side," Mirra decided.

"I'm not the enemy here," Roman declared, his handsome face rippling with annoyance.

"No, you're not. But you are the one in control, which puts things at a power imbalance," Jolie said.

"You three are among the most stunning and intelligent women I've ever had the pleasure of meeting," Roman said, his eyes landing on Avery again before darting away, leaving a little singe of heat on her skin. "I highly doubt I'm the one in power."

"He's good," Jolie decided.

"Nailed it," Mirra agreed.

"Strong answer," Avery said.

Roman threw up his hands. "I'll leave you three to figure out your world domination," he said with a smile, and trudged back up the beach.

"I like him," Mirra said, her blond braids blowing in the breeze.

"So do I. But he isn't for us."

"No… that's for certain."

"Why not?" Avery asked, genuinely curious. "I think he'd be lucky to get either of you, but still – why wouldn't you consider him?"

"Oh, I'd snatch him up in an instant; he's one of the good ones. But no, not for me. I can feel it here," Jolie said, touching her gut.

"How do you know that's the right feeling to trust? What if it's just nerves?" Avery asked, curious about how casually they trusted their instincts.

"Don't you follow your gut?" Mirra wondered.

"I don't. Not always. Well, sometimes." Avery sighed and pinched her nose. "I don't know. My brain is so active and practical that it constantly questions what I feel in my gut. If I'm not busy talking myself out of something, my sister is busy talking me into something else. And, despite myself, I can get railroaded pretty easily."

"Really? That surprises me." Jolie cast a look at her as if to say, I thought I'd judged you better.

"Well, where most people are concerned, I have a really solid backbone. Except my sister – I swear I just bend over backwards for her. I think it's really because I know she has my best interests at heart and that she loves me. I can't say that for everyone."

"I can see where that would lead to some confusion on trusting your inner wisdom. I can help, if you'd like," Mirra offered, her voice as melodic as the waves that moved closer to their feet.

"Help… what? Help me learn to trust my instincts? How?"

"Well, since we're your mentors on these challenges and what not, I can help you learn when it's your gut telling you something that's for your own good and when your brain's telling you something different."

"Won't that interfere with filming?"

"Does it matter?" Jolie laughed. "They film so much and cut it all down to one-hour increments. Most of the footage will end up deleted."

"I hope so," Avery said and the women laughed.

"You are a very reluctant participant."

"I feel like that's been my motto in life lately," Avery admitted, kicking at the water when a wave inched up the beach and touched her toe.

"Are you going to change that?" Mirra asked, reaching out to squeeze Avery's hand gently.

"I… you know what? I really should. That's a horrible thing to be – a reluctant participant. I mean, here I am on this beautiful island, having an experience that most won't ever get in their lives. Why am I picking it apart? I should embrace this."

"You should," Jolie said.

"I should," Avery agreed.

"You will," Mirra changed their language gently.

"Even better, Mirra. With your guidance, I will embrace this. Thanks for the pep talk, ladies. I have a lot to think about, but for now I think I'm going to sneak off to bed. I want a clear mind for the morning."

"Sweet dreams, Avery. We're excited to watch you

bloom," Mirra called as Avery walked away. Turning, she shot them a wave and smile and forced herself to walk cheerfully through the party, nodding and smiling at everyone before finding her way to her bedroom.

A reluctant participant, Avery thought. What a horrible epitaph that would be.

CHAPTER 11

"Remember, you're on camera."

Avery blinked her eyes open, her head fuzzy from the champagne the night before, and stared at the white planks that lined the ceiling of the room she was in. It took a moment for her brain to register just where exactly she was. Careful to keep the sheet pulled up to her shoulders lest a breast pop out of her loose sleep tank, Avery rolled to her side and looked across the room at Cherylynn.

"Thank you. I probably would have stretched and shown the world all my goods if you hadn't reminded me," Avery admitted.

"Don't I know it, girl. I swear I'd sleep in a sleeping bag with all those cameras watching us if it wasn't so dang hot here."

"At least we have air conditioning."

"That's a blessing, for sure," Cherylynn agreed.

"How was the rest of your night?" Avery asked,

pushing a tangle of curls out of her face and studying her friend, who didn't look any worse for wear.

"Honey, where did you disappear off to? I swear we had so much fun, dancing until the middle of the night. Savannah fell over and sloshed red wine all over Mindy's dress, and they almost had a straight-out cat fight. I thought I'd be wading into the mix and pulling women out by their hair."

"Huh. Can I say I'm not sorry I missed that?" Avery shifted on the bed. Fighting made her uncomfortable, even though she'd learned over the years how to stand her ground if she needed to. But she found most arguments to be tiresome and unnecessary.

"Sure, but you'll have to learn to view this stuff as one of two things – it's either entertainment or it's knowledge."

"How so?"

"Well, as the games begin, it's smart to know who's not in each other's good graces."

"Ah, strategy. I guess it would help if I had any clue who Mindy or Savannah are."

"Those are details that help in trying to win a game, yes." Cherylynn shook her blond hair out and laughed. "Don't worry, I'll give you the Cliff Notes version over breakfast. Suffice to say, alliances are being formed."

"But how does that even matter? I mean, doesn't Beckett vote? What will an alliance do?"

"Remember, for the first two challenges, the group can vote to bring someone back. So you want to make sure people like you, just in case you get voted off. A vote back could be a save for you."

"Okay, got it. Do you want the bathroom first?"

"If you don't mind?"

"No problem, go ahead." Avery wanted time to digest what Cherylynn had just told her. Since she'd arrived on the island, she had been largely resistant to this experience. But with her newfound decision to embrace it all, that would mean learning the rules of the game. She'd always excelled at board games as a child – well, at least those with very precise rules, like Monopoly. Here it would seem the rules were straight-forward, and yet the strategy behind it all was much more subtle. Not only would she have to manage the relationships and emotions of the women in the group, but also work to gain Beckett's admiration. Since Avery had never been particularly good at flirting, she decided to stick to something she could do – managing people. Silently thanking her project manager role at work, Avery smiled when Cherylynn bounded out of the bath-room in her towel.

"I'm sorry I left early last night. I promise I'll be better today. It was just the whole day of travel catching up with me; sometimes I need a moment to catch my bearings."

"I understand. I can't believe they filmed us the first day. They should know we'd all be exhausted from trav-eling. I think today will be fun though!"

"Did they tell you what was on the agenda?"

"The first challenge is today. They said we'll be on

the beach, so be sure to prepare to be in the sun, sand, and water."

"Okay. Loads of sunscreen. Let me check my notebook…" Avery pulled the little notebook from the bag by her bed and flipped through until she found an outfit labeled "Beach – Active – not lounging." Making sure her pajamas were where they were supposed to be on her body, Avery slipped from beneath the cool sheet and went to her dresser, where she'd done her best to arrange her clothes in the outfits Ruby had described. Finding her beach activewear, she pulled out a bright orange and white bikini with a full coverage bottom and a sporty tank-style top. Paired with simple denim cutoffs and a white crochet knit halter tank, it would allow Avery to move about or run, or whatever this challenge held, without feeling like all her bits and pieces were on display to the whole world.

"We need to be down to breakfast in ten minutes," Cherylynn said from where she was carefully applying her makeup in a little wicker mirror hanging over the dresser.

"Got it," Avery said. She raced into the bathroom, where she managed a quick shower and shave, brushed her teeth, and spent a good portion of that time applying liberal amounts of her reef-safe sunscreen. Giving it time to soak into her skin, she peered at herself in the mirror. Her hair, a riot of curls around her face, couldn't be tamed at this point, so she just ran some water on her hands and lightly bounced the curls into shape. She debated whether or not to put on some mascara, but finally decided against makeup. If they were going to be sweating on the beach and wearing sunglasses, what was the point? The last thing she needed was makeup running in her eyes and irritating them.

"You look great! All citrusy and whatnot." Cherylynn studied her, hands on hips, when Avery emerged from the bathroom.

"Thank you. I didn't do any makeup; think I'll be okay?"

Cherylynn gasped and brought her hand to her heart, pretending to struggle to breathe.

"Don't blaspheme around a Texan, Avery. You know we love our big hair and makeup."

"I know, but I'm just going to sweat it off anyway." Avery laughed at Cherylynn's wide eyes.

"Please tell me you've heard of this invention called waterproof mascara."

"I have. But does it matter if I have sunglasses on?"

"Yes. It matters. It always matters."

"I guess I'll just have to sacrifice and see what happens." Avery found herself laughing as they left the room, Cherylynn glancing back desperately toward her makeup bag.

"Are you sure you don't want me to just put a touch…"

"No, Cherylynn, I'm fine. We're going to be late," Avery said, dragging her friend down the hallway.

"I just don't know what to do with myself. Not wearing mascara! I can't get over it." Cherylynn shook her head sadly as if to say, 'You can't save them all.'

"Well, if I get kicked off, we'll know why," Avery teased.

Cherylynn gasped again. "Not yet. You can't leave me yet. I need you here."

"Who's leaving? Are you leaving?" A girl with brunette pigtails and bright blue baby-doll eyes looked at Avery in shock at the base of the stairs.

"Of course I'm not leaving," Avery quickly assured her before the rumor mill took off. "She's just having a mild heart attack over the fact that I didn't put mascara on this morning."

"You... didn't..." The woman's mouth dropped open and she blinked vaguely at Cherylynn.

"That's what I'm telling her, Mindy. She doesn't get it."

Ah, the Mindy of the cat fight the night before, Avery thought, and plastered a bright smile on her face.

"Hi, Mindy. I'm Avery. I'm sorry I missed meeting you last night."

"That's okay, it was a ridiculous night anyway. It was just my favorite dress, and you know how awful it is getting red wine out of white."

"I do," Avery said, though she wasn't sure she would threaten to come to blows with someone over it.

"Let's get some food before all the good stuff is picked over," Cherylynn said. Then, zeroing in on the buffet table set up on the other side of the expansive main room, she took off.

Avery, who enjoyed food as much as the next person, beelined after her, not wanting to repeat her hangry mood from yesterday. The croissants looked extra flaky and delicious, so she added one to her plate along with a scoop of fruit salad.

"Ewww," breathed a rail-thin woman next to her. "Carbs."

"Um, what? What's wrong with carbs?" Avery asked, but the woman just rolled her eyes and walked away from the food, filling up a cup of coffee from the tray at the end of the table.

"Carbs are the devil," Cherylynn supplied helpfully.

"Apparently. I guess I'll just eat mine in shame in the corner."

"No way. If you're going to eat carbs, then you'd better flaunt them and enjoy every damn bite," Cherylynn said, adding scrambled eggs and bacon to her plate.

"This is going to be a weird day, isn't it?"

"Oh yeah, it absolutely is, honey. But what's life without a little bit of weird?"

"Got it. Embrace the weird. I'm not putting my croissant back though."

"Don't you dare. Enjoy every last crumb of it."

CHAPTER 12

"*a* sand castle? Really?" Avery whispered.

Cherylynn kept a bright smile on her face while she spoke through her teeth. "A friggin' sand castle."

"How is this a challenge?" Avery wondered and then closed her mouth when Jack, the announcer, began talking again.

"That's right, ladies. We're keeping it easygoing and fun today with the simple challenge of building a sand-castle. You'll be separated into four groups of four, and will have to work together to build a castle. Each team will get one tool to use. That's all!"

"And does the best sand castle win?" Mindy asked, tugging on one of her pigtails and sending a flirtatious look at the camera.

"Beckett will be judging this round," Jack said, sweeping a hand out to motion for Beckett to step forward from the sideline. The women broke into applause at his arrival and Avery did her best to look like she gave a shit about him.

"That smile's a little scary, hon," Cherylynn whispered.

"I'll tone it down," Avery said, and dialed back the manic look a bit.

Beckett looked at ease today, in long board shorts, no shirt, and a hat promoting his surf camp. He smiled widely for the ladies and more than one of them cooed in response. Despite the ridiculousness of it all, Avery had to admit – he had some swagger to him.

"Good morning, ladies! I'm excited to get down and dirty in the sand with you today."

Gross, Avery thought, then gave herself a mental pat on the back for not saying that thought out loud. Jack ushered the group down to the sandy expanse of beach, and Avery took a moment to just breathe and take in the sights around her. She was a long way from home, and they certainly didn't have pretty palm trees and shockingly turquoise water like this in her neck of the woods. Feeling the warm sand under her toes, she lifted her face to the sun and enjoyed the kiss of the breeze on her cheeks for a moment. Though she loved her job, it was nice to not be staring at a computer screen right now. Returning to the moment, she opened her eyes and fell in line as the group came to a stop in the hardpacked sand by the water. Grateful for her sunglasses and copious amounts of sunscreen, she bit back a smile as more than one girl wiped sweat from her face.

"We'll just split you up where you're standing,"

Jack said, and Avery was glad to have stopped next to Cherylynn and Mindy. Lisette rounded out their group, and they smiled at each other as though to say, 'We're all just friends here having a little frolic on the beach.'

"And here are each of your tools."

Avery raised an eyebrow as Jack handed out a single hand shovel to one group, a pail to another, and a mini rake to the third. Their own group, the fourth, received a turret-shaped bucket. Then, smiling, he stepped back. Beckett could barely conceal his amusement as all the women looked sadly at their little tools and realized they'd have to use their hands to build something.

"Ready? Set? Go!"

Squeals erupted as each team dove into the sand and began to plan. The arguments started instantly, and the cameras circled like vultures.

"What are we supposed to do with just this little turret?" Lisette pouted, kneeling prettily in the sand. Avery wanted to high-five her for knowing the word, but kept that particular impulse to herself.

"Use it to dig," Cherylynn said. She grabbed it from her hands, and began scooping buckets of sand out to form a pile.

"But what kind of castle are we making?"

"A pretty one?" Cherylynn suggested as she dumped more sand in a pile.

"A lumpy pile of sand hardly looks pretty," Lisette pointed out, her mouth in a perpetual pout and eyes scanning for the cameras. When her face changed to a soft and dreamy smile, Avery knew that Beckett must be approaching.

"Ladies, how's it going over here?" Beckett crouched next to Avery, his muscled thigh casually brushing hers, and Avery reminded herself to play nice.

"Good morning, Beckett. Did you have fun last night?"

"I did, thanks for asking. I missed you though." Beckett gave her a long look out of his cool blue eyes, and Avery couldn't help but feel that the move was a practiced one.

"I'm sorry. Jet lag and all..." Avery shrugged, breaking their look and studying the increasingly large pile of sand that Cherylynn was building. "What's the plan, Cherylynn?"

"I'm trying to make a big hole so we can have a moat," Cherylynn supplied.

"Why do we need a moat?" Mindy asked, her eyes on Beckett.

"Every castle needs a moat," Beckett said, and Avery watched a flash of annoyance cross Mindy's face.

"Of course, duh. Let's build a moat!" Mindy said, faking cheer.

"That's what I'm doing," Cherylynn bit out.

Avery pressed her lips together to hide her smile.

"Well, my moat is going to be better."

"Says who? You aren't even doing anything. You're just sitting there."

"Well, you have the only tool."

"You have hands, don't you?"

"It's not like they'll do much. We need more tools."

"Maybe we could ask the other team if we can use their shovel?" Lisette offered, having moved around the pit to crouch by Beckett. She'd already placed her hand on his knee and Beckett was drinking in the view down her barely-there bikini top.

"Yeah, like anyone's going to agree to give up their tools. This is a competition, remember?" Mindy grimaced, her hands deep in the sand. Every time she pulled a handful out, she looked in dismay at her manicure and shot daggers with her eyes at Cherylynn.

Avery had a pretty good idea where this was going. She'd seen it more than enough times onsite at her projects – without anyone giving clear direction, everything fell into chaos. Which was likely what the producers wanted, Avery thought.

She glanced around for Roman. Not finding him right away, she tuned into the arguments erupting on all sides of her while the cameras circled gleefully. A bead of sweat trickled down her back and she wanted nothing more than to be away from all these increasingly angry women.

Standing up, she put her hands on her hips and surveyed the scene. None of the groups had gotten much further than the others, and it reminded Avery of a bunch of toddlers about to have a meltdown in the sandbox. Before anyone could throw their toys and have a tantrum, Avery surprised everyone by clapping her hands loudly. Ignoring the cameras that swung towards her, she stepped into the middle of the group.

"Hi everyone! Listen… this is all kind of a mess. We all have tools the other groups need to build their castles. Since Jack didn't state that each group had to make their own castle, I vote we all work together to build one big castle. What does everyone think about that?"

Cheers greeted her and Avery found herself grinning back, and falling naturally into her project manager role.

"Okay, let's make this easier. Who wants to collect shells?" A few hands shot up from the group. "Great, you all go over there and start collecting shells."

"I like to dig," Cherylynn offered, gesturing at the large pile of sand by her side as evidence.

"Great. Diggers over here."

"What about rocks? Or sea grasses for the garden?" Lisette offered.

"Fabulous. Interior designers – over here." Avery motioned for the women to form groups.

"Structural design?" Avery asked hopefully, and was surprised to see two hands raised. "Great, with me. Let's build the prettiest sandcastle this island has seen!"

Everyone whooped and ran off in their groups, and what had been almost pandemonium moments before turned into cheerful chatter as each woman found her happy place on the sand.

Turning, Avery caught Roman smiling at her from where he leaned on a palm tree in the distance. Biting back a smile, as she knew she wasn't supposed to acknowledge him, she crouched in the sand near Cherylynn's moat. If it felt nice to see Roman's smile of approval, Avery wasn't going to admit it to herself. Nope, not in the slightest did it matter what that man thought of her.

"Nicely done." Beckett ran a hand down her back stopping it just at her waist as he crouched next to her. "I like a woman who knows how to take charge."

Annoyed that he was touching her without permission, but knowing the cameras were on her and she couldn't just shrug him off, Avery shifted gently, reaching for a stick one of the women had brought over and moving herself out of his range.

"I kind of fall into it by default. Someone has to oversee things on my projects."

"What do you do?"

"Environmental engineer," Avery said and caught his look of surprise.

"I'm an architect," said one of the women who had come to join Avery.

"And I'm a carpenter," the other woman said, and Avery couldn't stop the laugh that bubbled out at Beckett's look of surprise.

"Looks like I have my dream team," Avery said. Then, turning to the two women and neatly cutting Beckett out, she bent and began to draw in the sand with her stick. "Now, how many levels do we want on this castle? And should there be a drawbridge?"

It might not have been the prettiest sandcastle ever made, but by the time they were done with it, the entire group had done something they were proud of. Cherylynn shocked Avery by almost barreling her over with an effusive hug.

"It's beautiful! I'm so glad you took charge."

"He didn't say we had to make separate castles." Nonetheless, Avery felt her cheeks heat at the praise.

"I know! I didn't even think about it. But look – it's so pretty! There's shells in the courtyard, and seagrass bridges, and the moat looks amazing! I'm so proud of us." Cherylynn bounced on her heels, and the rest of the group all came over to hug Avery.

By the time they had finished, Avery was shocked to realize that tears threatened. She didn't even want to be a part of this group – so why did it matter if they approved of her?

Avery thought of her sister, and how'd she spent much of her life letting Ruby steamroll her. Maybe she was just always seeking approval. The problem was, the only person she really wanted approval from was herself.

"Congratulations, ladies!" Jack strolled up, and even though he put a smile on for the camera, Avery could tell he was annoyed that they had succeeded in their challenge. It would make for better TV if they'd fallen apart, but Avery was proud they hadn't all stooped that low. She could only imagine it would get worse as the stakes got higher, but for Round One, winning this challenge as a group actually felt quite good. "You've made a lovely castle and you are all winners!"

The group cheered, but Avery waited for the other shoe to drop.

"So, this particular challenge was about compromise and working together. These traits are incredibly valuable in a relationship. Beckett was making his marks as he toured around, and each of you have been scored on those traits today. We'll start our elimination now."

The man really enjoyed his power trip, Avery thought as she watched a sliver of glee pass over Jack's face before he schooled his expression. Ignoring him, she turned to Cherylynn.

"What happens when you get eliminated?"

"I think you just full on leave. Like today. Pack your bag, go to the airport."

"What if there isn't a flight out?" Avery asked, wondering just how many flights arrived at this little island on a daily basis.

"I'm sure they'd put you up somewhere. But no more filming."

"Jeez, that's got to be weird. What an awkward situation this is," Avery muttered, and looked for Roman in the crowd. He stood in the background, consulting a clipboard. He looked good today, wearing loose board shorts, a faded grey t-shirt, and aviators shading his eyes. She wanted to see his eyes again, Avery realized. She swung her attention back to Jack.

"Now, ladies, this first challenge is a tough one – unfortunately, four of you will be out."

A gasp went through the group and Avery felt the mood shift from one of cohesion to one of suspicion. Nobody wanted to be the first to go, and the careful alliances they'd built during their team project disintegrated at their feet.

"Beckett... if you'd like?" Jack stood back and gestured to Beckett, who stepped forward with his most disarming smile on his face.

Clapping his hands together and shrugging sheepishly, he kicked at the sand a little, looking down and biting his lip before leveling his gaze on them. Everything about his demeanor felt practiced to Avery, and she wondered if he'd received training for this role or he was just used to putting on a show.

"Ladies, honestly, this is a tough one. Picking four of you to go when I've barely had a chance to get to know you is... rough, to say the least. But those are the rules and I must abide by them. Please know, I'm only picking based on what I saw in the challenge. Being a team player is really important to me and I want to be with someone who I can work together with. It's not easy running my camp, and I need people who can help me in that endeavor, not hinder me."

Avery raised an eyebrow at this. He seemed to mention his camp as often as he could, which suggested to her that he was in this for publicity. He didn't honestly think that these women would give up their jobs to come work at his camp, did he?

"That being said – and again, I hate having to do this – I'm eliminating Mindy, Cherylynn, Grace, and Delia."

"No!" Avery gasped, while the other women all made similar shell-shocked responses.

"I... I was the one doing the work from the beginning." Cherylynn clutched Avery's hand.

"It must have been that little tiff you had with Mindy."

"Then Mindy should go. She's the one starting fights with everyone all the time," Cherylynn said, and for the first time Avery saw her friend's good spirits waver.

"Don't worry – we can vote you back, remember? I'll make this happen," Avery promised.

Cherylynn squeezed her arm. "Do you think you can?"

"I'll do my damnedest," Avery said. "Because I certainly don't think I'll last here without you."

CHAPTER 13

"I can't be the first to go," Cherylynn wailed. They were back in their rooms, having been given a break to prepare for their night ceremony. It seemed they were meant to spend some time discussing if they would vote for a woman to stay.

"I mean, technically you wouldn't be the first, because there are four of you," Avery supplied, then winced when Cherylynn shot her a glare. "Sorry, that was rude of me."

"No, you're right. But still, it stings."

"What can I do to help? I don't think I'll last here without you, I really don't," Avery said, plopping onto her bed and throwing her hand over her forehead. Perhaps it was a bit dramatic, but she really needed Cherylynn to stay and be her sounding board.

"Can you go talk to the others and put a good word in for me?"

"Of course, I'll go right now," Avery said, getting

back up. Impulsively, she bent and hugged Cherylynn. Avery wasn't one for open displays of affection, but she had really taken a liking to Cherylynn. "It'll be okay. If you get voted off, maybe I can volunteer my place instead. You want this more than I do."

"That might be the sweetest thing anyone's ever offered to do for me." Cherylynn blinked up at her and squeezed Avery's hand. "But I couldn't possibly accept that from you, hon. Sure, this stings a bit, but it's not the end of the world. I doubt I'll win this; I just didn't want to be the first to go. I'm made of tougher stuff than this. Just let me have a little cry, then I'll kick the dirt off my boots and ride on."

"That's the spirit. Let me go talk to the others. I'll try to get a read on what's happening."

"You go on without me…" Cherylynn gasped, grabbing at her throat and collapsing dramatically on her bed as Avery left the room, chuckling.

She followed the sound of voices coming from the lower floor. Descending the stairs, she stopped short to see Roman leaning in the doorway on his telephone.

"I love you," Roman said into the phone. "You're the best woman I know." Hanging up, he turned and caught Avery's look.

"Hello. How goes it today?" Roman asked, walking forward until he stood close to Avery – too close, in her opinion, for someone who was just professing his love to another woman.

"It goes. How's your girlfriend?" Avery asked before she could stop herself. She immediately wanted to take the words back. She didn't care if he had a girl-friend, a wife, or a harem of women. It was Beckett she was supposed to be focused on – not this cranky producer.

"Jealous?" A wide smile split Roman's face and Avery imagined pushing him into the pool the next time he walked past it.

"Not in the slightest. Just making small talk. If you can ask invasive questions about my life, I don't see why I can't ask some about yours."

"First, asking you questions is part of the deal you signed up for. Secondly, asking you if you believe in soulmates or follow a particular religion isn't neces-sarily invasive. If I wanted to be invasive, I could ask you when was the last time a man made your legs shake from hours of loving your body."

Heat flushed her cheeks, and Avery cursed her redhead's skin while a long liquid pull heated her core.

"That's really none of your business," Avery said, sounding prim even to herself. She licked her suddenly dry lips.

"Exactly. It is none of my business. Which is why I don't ask you questions like that. Although from the looks of it, the idea seems to intrigue you." A sliver of a smile slipped across Roman's face, but his eyes stayed serious as they held hers.

"I… well, I mean, of course it intrigues me," Avery sputtered. "What woman doesn't like hours of pleasure visited upon her body? You'd be crazy to think someone wouldn't find that appealing."

Roman laughed, and Avery found herself smirking up at him. He had a remarkable ability to go from annoying to charming in seconds.

"How's Cherylynn?" Roman asked, neatly changing the subject – and also not answering her question, Avery realized.

"Not happy. She'll be fine, but she doesn't want to be the first to go."

"I don't blame her. Being the first always has a sting to it. Are you going to vote to have her stay?"

"That's the plan. I need to go talk to the other women and see what the deal is." Avery looked over to the couches, where many of the women had gathered. Plates and cups of coffee were littered about, and the conversation looked to be growing heated.

"Good luck," Roman said. Stepping back, he did his best to fade into the corner, reminding Avery that they were indeed still being filmed. Shaking her hair back, she did her best not to look at the cameras and went to join the other women.

"I think Delia should definitely go. She hasn't been friendly with anyone," Lisette said, stretching a tanned leg in front of her. She seemed to have more interest in examining her pedicure than in the fate of the woman she was discussing.

"Hi." Avery dropped down next to her and nodded to the other women. None of the eliminated women were around, but Avery wondered if they were hovering in the stairwell above, listening as their future was decided. "How does this work exactly? Will we all vote together? Or do we all put ballots in? Do we have to decide in advance?"

"There'll be a dramatic ceremony tonight, and we'll all cast a ballot on who should stay," Lisette supplied. "They'll count them and one person can stay."

"How does everyone currently feel?" Avery asked carefully.

"Everyone's torn. There's no real way to choose who stays." Lisette was now examining her hair and frowning slightly at what must be a split end.

"Well, I think there is. It doesn't necessarily have to only be based on who is friends with whom. But what about the person who's been the kindest? Or someone you feel you can trust? I mean... I heard there was a fight last night. What happened there?"

"That was with Mindy," Lisette said, and the other girls began to nod in agreement.

"I heard it didn't go so well," Avery said, choosing her words carefully.

"It didn't. Mindy was awful," one of the women said, and the others all were quick to agree.

"Plus she fought with Cherylynn today too," Lisette said, then began telling the group how bitchy Mindy had been during sandcastle building.

One down, Avery thought. She let the others talk about the two other women. She hadn't had much time with them, so she couldn't offer an opinion one way or the other, and she wanted to let things go naturally so it didn't seem like she was scheming.

"Avery, you're rooming with Cherylynn. What are your thoughts on her?"

"Honestly, she's been really helpful to me," Avery admitted, looking around at the other women, an earnest expression on her face. "I've felt a bit out of my comfort zone here – this is the first time I've ever done anything like this. She's been really good at making sure we have fun and enjoy this experience to the fullest. Because, let's be honest here, ladies, how often do we get to do something like this in a beautiful place like Siren Island? Cherylynn has really helped me to appreciate where we are, and to take each moment as something really special."

"It is special," Lisette agreed. "I've done a couple of these shows, but this is by far the prettiest location, and with the best bunch of girls I could ask for."

A few women sniffled and Avery blinked in shock as, one after another, they began to cry, pulling each other into hugs and talking about how grateful they were for each other and this moment in time they'd been gifted. The cameras circled, eating it up, while Avery looked on in confusion. Were they really at the tears-and-hugging-each-other point already?

"Should I start singing 'Kumbaya'?" Avery asked and laughter broke out from the group.

"We like you, Avery," Lisette deciding, slinging an arm over her shoulder. "I might even help you get onto Instagram. I'll design your profile for you. It'll be great."

"Great…" Avery said, panicking a bit.

"I promise. You'll love it."

"Too bad we don't have our phones," Avery said, hoping to drop the subject.

"That's fine, I'll set it up at the end. I'll Skype with you and we'll figure it out. I don't mind taking people under my wing."

Avery wasn't entirely sure she wanted to be taken under Lisette's wing, but in the interest of playing nice and making friends, she half-heartedly agreed. Figuring she'd done what she could to blow the winds of favor in Cherylynn's direction without creating too much controversy, Avery went to forage for snacks to bring up to the room for Cherylynn.

"You played that nicely," Roman commented from his new perch on the kitchen counter. Avery jumped – she had been so focused on the snack basket in front of her that she hadn't seen him.

"I didn't 'play' anything. I just don't want Cherylynn to leave."

"From the outside, it looks like you neatly maneuvered everyone to where you wanted them to be."

"I've worked in project management for years. There's a knack to getting people to agree on something. Mainly, you have to let them think it was their own idea. I didn't do anything wrong, I was just laying out some of the facts."

"I know. I didn't say you did anything wrong." Roman watched her carefully as she nibbled her lower lip, feeling the need to defend herself.

"I don't think helping people make an informed

decision is doing anything bad," Avery mumbled, digging through the basket and pulling out some granola bars and a few packets of chips.

"It isn't bad. I admire how your brain works. You must be good at your job," Roman said, almost too smoothly.

Avery stopped to look up at him. "And now you're maneuvering me." She raised an eyebrow at him.

He held up his hands in the air. "Hey now, it's not my first rodeo having an argument with a woman. I find it's best to smooth any ruffled feathers I can."

"I'm not... my feathers aren't ruffled," Avery exclaimed, shaking her head at him. "Well, maybe they're getting ruffled, now that you've said that. God, didn't we talk about you working on being an asshole?"

"How was anything I said being an asshole?" Roman crossed his arms over his chest and studied her.

"You're just... ugh, I don't know." Avery wanted to smack the counter, but her hands were full of snacks. "It's not that you're outright being an asshole right now. It's just – little comments that come across as condescending. Like you have to just walk around placating women all the time because we're some sort of irrational beasts that'll fly off the handle at any given moment." It didn't help her point that her voice was rising or the fact that her face was flushed. Realizing she might sound a bit hypocritical, Avery took a deep breath.

"I –" Roman began.

"Listen, I'm just sensitive to the whole 'there there'

mentality that a lot of men adopt. I'm in a fairly male-dominated field and it puts my back up when people act like women are these fragile beings incapable of handling ourselves or our projects. This isn't all you; it's something I deal with constantly on the job site."

"That's fair. I'm sorry. I shouldn't lump you in with a lot of the women I come across either. From what I can gather you're highly intelligent, seem competent, and I enjoy speaking to you. Unlike many of the women here. I'm sorry, I really shouldn't bait you. It must be an instinctive thing from back on the days of the playground – you know, boys needling the girls they…" Roman trailed off.

Both of Avery's eyebrows shot clear to her hairline when she realized what he had almost said. "The girls they what?" she asked sweetly, enjoying the flash of emotions that rushed over his face.

"They think are cool," Roman finished quickly. He hopped off the counter, saying, "I have to check the production tapes from this morning."

Without another word, he strode off, leaving Avery with an armful of snacks and a brain whirling with questions.

CHAPTER 14

"*L*adies, please cast your votes."

Roman watched as his cameramen circled the room, carefully filming each woman's facial expressions, zooming in over their shoulders to see what name they were writing on the slips of paper they'd been handed. His crew worked together efficiently, and barely needed direction from him. They'd already done a few rounds of filming these types of shows with him, and knew what the money shots were.

In spite of his best efforts to not look over at Avery, Roman found his eyes drifting to where she sat, nibbling her lower lip, a worried expression in her huge eyes. He wondered if she had any idea that she bit her lower lip when she was worried, or just how intoxicating her eyes became when she was working out a problem in that fascinating brain of hers. No wonder she'd come across a lot of opposition in her field of work. Roman could only imagine how difficult it would be to sit across the desk from a woman like her and stay focused on the task at hand. He could hardly manage it now, and he was barely in the same room as her.

He'd stay just long enough to see her smile, Roman decided, then slip away for a breather. These shoots were non-stop and if he didn't take some time to himself, he'd burn out before the show was over. It wasn't that he minded working long hours – it was that he had a hard time being around people talking incessantly for hours on end. It was part of what had driven him to explore the wilds of so many different countries. Not only was he determined to bring about real and actionable change with his documentaries, but he also loved the peace that nature brought to his soul.

Avery glowed in the candlelight, Roman thought, his eyes drawn helplessly back to where she sat, her hand clasped in Cherylynn's. Tonight she wore a dusky green slip dress, her hair bound back in a loose braid with curls popping loose, and simple swingy gold earrings. Perhaps it was because she tried less that she stood out more, Roman mused as he scanned the rest of the women, who were done up in all the flash and glitz they could find. In theory, a woman like Lisette would be considered traditionally more beautiful than Avery, with her model-like build, stunning face, and long sweep of artfully tousled hair. But the substance was missing, and that was what kept drawing Roman back to Avery. There was something about her that made him want to peel back the next layer and see what made her tick.

A smile flashed across her face like a flash of lightning illuminating a dark beach, and Roman lost his breath for a moment. Then the women were hugging, and Roman knew that Avery had won her quest to keep Cherylynn on the show.

For now.

Easing back onto the deck, Roman turned and followed the walkway past the swaying palm trees to find the beach. He needed to connect with the earth and get his head on straight, he thought. He kicked his sandals off and wandered down the beach, each step pressing thickly into damp sand at the water's edge. Only when he was far enough away from the villa did he finally stop. Finding a clump of boulders to sit on, he leaned back to look up at the night sky.

A cooling rush of calm pushed through him as he breathed deeply, focusing on the stars, and allowed himself to find his center once more.

He'd promised his mother on the phone earlier that he was fine, but now he wondered if he really was. She worried, he knew, that he wandered too far and too long, and would never settle down. But settling down for him was akin to death, and he'd yet to find a woman who wanted the same things he did. His past relationships had proven that, Roman thought. He crossed his arms over his chest, blowing out a breath, and kicked his toes in the water. Each of his girlfriends had enjoyed the traveling lifestyle for a while. But eventually they had all craved the same thing – a house, a routine, and a family. Nothing wrong with that, but it wasn't for him.

A song whispered across the waves, an invitation,

and Roman had hopped off his perch and was half in the water before he realized what he was doing. He stopped and held his breath as a hauntingly beautiful voice slipped across the water. The notes slid through him, tendrils of lust and longing entwining themselves around his heart until tears pricked his eyes. In that moment, he would have given his life just so the song would never end. When it cut short, it was like a knife sliced through him and an ache filled the space where the music had been. Swiping at his eyes, he stared out to sea as the water rushed around his waist.

"Going for a swim?"

Roman turned to see Irma standing on the sand, seemingly illuminated from within; her white dress glowed around her and her hair danced in the breeze. Bracelets jingled at her wrists as she motioned for him to come back from the depths. Heart pounding, Roman turned to look back out over the water, before shaking his head and forcing himself to walk back toward the beach. Each step felt like quicksand and he wanted nothing more than to dive back into the water and swim until he found the ethereal and haunting voice that had beckoned to him from across the sea.

"I... I'm not sure what I'm doing," Roman admitted when he finally stood in front of Irma, saltwater dripping from his legs. Reaching up, Irma put a hand to his chest and a cool rush of calmness zipped through him, so strong that he had to acknowledge that she'd just done something to him.

But what was that something?

"You heard them," Irma said, starlight glinting from her eyes.

"I… I felt like I was entranced," Roman said. "I was half in the water before the song was finished."

"Didn't you make a rule about nobody going in the water after dark?" Irma teased. She took his hand, gently easing him back to the boulder where he'd just been sitting.

"I did. I had. I don't know," Roman said, shaking his head as if to clear the last dredges of the intoxicating song from his mind, but he knew the notes would be forever emblazoned on his soul. "What… what was that?"

"The sirens," Irma said, tilting her head to study his response.

"The… sirens. Right. Siren Island, I get it," Roman almost chuckled, but then thought better of it. He'd been trained to be open-minded, and to explore the unknown. While this was certainly unknown territory, he wasn't just going to dismiss Irma as being silly. He'd traveled the world enough to know that there were many things that defied explanation. This could be one of them.

"Do you though?" Irma asked.

"Do I what?"

"Get it, as you say." A smile slipped across Irma's face and Roman found himself once again admiring her almost otherworldly beauty.

"Well, this is named Siren Island. I suppose it would make sense if there were sirens to be found here."

"But do you actually believe in things like sirens and

mermaids? Or do you think they are nothing but tall tales told on sailing ships after one too many rounds of rum?"

"I honestly can say that I've never given the existence of sirens or mermaids much thought before," Roman said, figuring it was a fair enough answer. He wasn't one to dismiss something just because he hadn't seen proof of it one way or the other.

"You're open to the possibility then?"

"Considering the depths of the ocean and the unknowns of this universe, yes, I'm open to the possibility that sirens are real," Roman said, wiping a hand over his face.

"That's fair-minded of you," Irma decided, nudging his arm a little with her own. "I like a man who doesn't immediately dismiss things he doesn't totally understand."

"I like to seek answers. I'm an explorer and an adventurer. I don't know what it was that I just heard, but it was possibly the most intoxicatingly beautiful song I've ever had the pleasure of hearing. I don't honestly know that I'll ever be the same." Roman pressed a hand to his chest and took a deep breath, feeling the remnants of the music still embedded in him. "What did you do to me just now?"

"What did you feel?" Irma asked, her eyes bright and curious as she looked up at him.

"It felt like you sent cool water through me and calmed my nerves."

"Ah, interesting. You *are* open. I wondered," Irma said.

Roman just stared blankly at her. "You gotta give me more here, Irma," he finally said.

She laughed, the sound like a tinkling of bells dancing across the waves. "Open to energies, that's all. I just gave you a little healing energy. You looked a bit shell-shocked, standing fully clothed in the water. I was almost convinced you were going to swim out to follow their song."

"I almost did. And you keep saying 'their.' What do you know about these sirens? Obviously there's something more to the story if you can hear them, and you seem to know about them. I know I didn't just dream that, and I haven't had a drop of alcohol tonight. Unless someone slipped some drugs in my drink, I'm absolutely sober and completely aware that I just had some sort of otherworldly experience."

"I'm assuming you've read the history of Siren Island? You know about the young couple in love and the heartbreak because two worlds kept them apart?"

"I did read the stories, yes. I always read up on where I'm going to visit," Roman said. "But I'll admit I thought they were just fables. You know, myths interwoven with history through the ages."

"Why did you assume that they were just myths?"

"Because mermaids aren't real," Roman said automatically.

"Aren't they?" Irma asked, her eyes on his.

Roman felt like the blood slowed in his veins, and the beat of his heart thumped loudly in his ears.

"Are you saying they are?"

"I'm asking what you believe."

"Like I said, I've never given it much thought. I think that since there's so little evidence mermaids exist, my assumption has always been that they don't."

"Why do you say there is little evidence?"

"I mean, there's no pictures. No video. No scientific studies done on how they would breathe or exist in the ocean. What do they eat? How do they mate? Do they form societies? What are their rules? Is there a hierarchy like in wolf packs? Just, you know, about a ton of questions to be answered."

"Yet for thousands of years, in almost every culture or society that has lived by the water or been seafaring, there are tales of mermaids. Stories abound through the centuries about mermaids. Sirens and mermaids are woven into the fabric of the myths and legends of the ocean. Do you think those stories have come across time from imagination only? Before the internet? Before societies even knew there were other humans across the world from them? It wasn't like people were consistently working together, thousands of years ago, to create a big myth about mermaids that would forever implant itself as one big practical joke for generations to come. Don't you think that, when you look at the data as a whole across all populations, there are too many accounts and eyewitnesses to dismiss?"

"Hmmm." Roman was at a loss for words as his mind whirled with the possibilities.

"It's easier to explain away something you don't know, something that makes you uncomfortable, as just, you know, a dolphin in the water, than it is to entertain the possibility of something more. But I feel like you wouldn't do that. Not really… not when you've just had an experience like you did. What do you say, then, Roman? Are you Team Skeptical or Team Believer?"

"I…well, I can't dismiss what just happened to me. But I'm also a skeptic, just in the fact that I like to gather data about what I don't understand."

"That's fair. I can offer you more data. Or send you to a lovely store downtown that has some books and information on our local legends. But tell me…" Irma stepped forward and pressed her hand to Roman's chest. "What do you feel?"

"I feel like I was given a great gift tonight," Roman said, surprising himself, and yet he knew it to be true. Even if he'd been a fool and strode right into the ocean, ready to swim into darkness to find the one singing that incredible song, he knew he'd been given a rare glimpse into something he didn't fully understand.

"It is a gift," Irma said, stepping back, a smile on her face. "Use it wisely."

"Irma… what are you?" Roman whispered, his gaze trailing over the glow that seemed to hover over her skin. In the light of the moon she easily could have been a mermaid or a sea goddess, the waves dancing at her feet.

"I'm an everywoman, Roman. Of the sea, the earth, and the stars. She who walks the land and dances on the water."

Roman had no words as Irma all but floated away, as ethereal and lithe on the beach as the everywoman she described. For a moment Roman felt his heart stop as the song, now embedded in his soul, rose from the water once more. It stopped as quickly as it had begun, leaving Roman aching for something... more. When an image of Avery flashed through his mind, he shoved it away, instead lingering by the water, hoping against hope that the sirens would sing for him once more.

CHAPTER 15

"What do you think the challenge will be today? Climbing a tree to get a coconut?" Avery asked Cherylynn the next morning as they got ready for another day of filming. The night before had been draining, with tearful goodbyes to the three women who had to leave – though why the girl who had fought with Mindy over the red wine incident was suddenly hugging her and crying about her leaving was beyond Avery. The level of fakeness in this group was certainly rising.

"Oh god, I hope not. If they demean us with another dumb exercise, I'm going to be annoyed," Cherylynn said, teasing her blond roots with a comb.

"I don't feel like they're setting the bar very high on these so-called challenges," Avery said, settling back onto the bed to watch Cherylynn put herself together. She'd already put on her Ruby-approved outfit and had thrown her curls up in a high ponytail. Though Cherylynn had made tsking noises at her lack of makeup, Avery didn't really care. All that mattered was that she had a healthy dose of sunscreen covering her and that she was mentally prepared for whatever the producers threw at them today.

Thinking of the producers, Avery wondered where Roman had gone last night. She'd seen him briefly, filming the beginning of the goodbye ceremony, but then he'd disappeared. Did he get to take breaks while filming? Wasn't it his job to be on top of what the cameramen were doing? Annoyed with herself for even thinking of him, she tuned back into Cherylynn's chatter.

"Beckett looked hot last night. What do you think of him?"

"I think... well, I think he seems very nice," Avery said carefully.

"He does seem nice. And hot," Cherylynn offered.

"I also think he might just be on here to promote his business."

"Duh, that's what most people come on here for," Cherylynn laughed, not fussed that Beckett might be using these women as a tool for promotion.

"But... doesn't that bother you? Aren't we supposed to be falling in love and all that?"

"I think everyone is here to play the game."

"I just... doesn't this all feel a little weird? The fakeness of it all?" Avery wondered as she plucked at a loose thread at the edge of her shorts.

"Not if you know what you're getting into from the

beginning. I think where it goes wrong is when people don't have the appropriate expectations. If anyone comes on here truly looking for love, their feelings will probably get hurt in the long run. But if you manage your expectations – play the game and see where it goes – you'll come out of this none the worse for wear, your heart in one piece, maybe much richer, but overall you'll have something cool to add to your list of life experiences."

"I admire your ability to look at things that way. I haven't watched enough reality shows to understand if people are really thinking they'll fall in love or not. But from all the crying and carrying on, it seems like a lot of people get their feelings hurt."

"I suspect a lot of it is their egos getting hurt, hon, not their hearts," Cherylynn observed.

Avery marveled at her – this Texas straight-shooter who dropped advice bombs like a mini-Yoda.

"I guess looking like a fool on national television has to sting a bit," Avery admitted as she stood and followed Cherylynn out of the room.

They trailed behind the other girls leaving their rooms, down the deathtrap of a staircase, and out to the pool deck where Jack, Beckett, and Roman already waited. Avery immediately noticed that Roman was looking at her, but she couldn't read his expression; his eyes were covered once more by his aviator sunglasses. He seemed tense today, and she wondered why – or why she felt like she could read that energy from him across the pool.

"Good morning, ladies," Jack announced, signaling the beginning of another day of filming. Avery glanced longingly at the coffee station behind her, but straightened her shoulders and placed a smile on her face for the cameras. "We hope you got a good night's rest after the events of last night. Cherylynn, congratulations again on making the cut to stay."

The group cheered as Cherylynn smiled and performed a dramatic bow.

"Today we're sending you off on a bit of an adventure," Jack said with a smile. Avery noticed he was careful with his words – never revealing too much. She'd picked up on that yesterday, when he'd neatly avoided answering questions from the group. "You'll be able to pack a bag to bring with you on this adventure, and I'd say plan for an overnight. That means bring your glasses, contacts – anything that is vitally important to you for an overnight stay."

"Where are we going?" one woman piped up.

Jack just leveled a look at her. "You'll find out more about your adventure as you go along," he said evenly, and turned to Beckett.

"Ladies, I'll be joining you on your adventure, to get to know you each a little better," Beckett said. He looked rested this morning. "The more time we spend together, the easier I'll be able to see which one of you lovely ladies is the one for me."

Great, Avery thought, but kept the comment to herself.

"Is this an outdoor adventure?" Lisette asked.

"It is an outdoor adventure, so you'll want to bring what you think is necessary for the climate here."

The women were dismissed to pack and get ready for their day, and they immediately began discussing their outfits. Avery beelined it to the snack basket and loaded her bag with granola bars. Filling her reusable water bottle, she stopped by the coffee station to fuel herself with caffeine for the day ahead.

"Good morning, Avery," Beckett said at her side.

Avery turned to smile at him. Technically he'd been nothing but nice to her, and she needed to put on a show for him.

"Good morning, Beckett. Are you excited to explore a bit of the island today?" Avery asked.

"I am. They flew me in right before filming started so I haven't had much time to look around. It seems pretty sick though."

Avery hesitated for a moment, then remembered that West Coast people used 'sick' to mean 'cool.'

"It does. Plus a change of scenery will be nice. How are you getting on? Is it a lot to remember everyone's names and keep up with it all?" Avery genuinely wondered how he managed.

"Not too bad. I'm used to remembering a whole slew of names each week as we get new kids in at camp, so this isn't too rough for me. I think it's more trying to decide who's being fake and who's being real," Beckett admitted, leaning one hip against the counter as he studied her.

"Ah, you can sense that as well? I wondered how

you would know," Avery said. She was surprised that he had picked up on the acting skills of some of the women. She'd found some men to be blinded by beauty.

"Let's just say that I have no illusions about why many of the women are here. I'm doing my best to cut through all that and find out more about each woman."

"Best of luck on that one." Avery found herself laughing up at him.

"I'll need it. Why are you here, Avery?" Beckett smiled at her, softening his inquiry.

"Honestly? Because I'd been stuck in a rut and needed to be pushed out of my comfort zone. I'm not sure this is the exact way I wanted to do it, but nevertheless, here I am."

"That's probably the first honest answer I've heard to that question." Beckett laughed and looked around the room before his gaze landed back on her.

"I'm sorry, I don't mean to be hurtful," Avery said, quickly realizing she probably should have said she was looking for love, or something along those lines. "But I do think it might be tricky to learn to love someone under these circumstances."

"I do too. But at the very least, maybe I'll be able to determine if I have a strong attraction and a liking for someone. I think that could eventually blossom into love after the cameras are gone, don't you?"

"I... I truly hadn't thought about it like that." Avery was surprised by Beckett's introspection. Perhaps there was more to this one than met the eye, she thought as she added some cream to her coffee.

"It's a starting point. And hey, if it does work out, you'd have a really cool 'how we met' story to tell your children." Beckett smiled at her and straightened, nodding at Jack, who was waving to him from across the room. "I have to go. See you later, Avery. I enjoyed talking to you."

"You too, Beckett," Avery said, and blushed when he dropped a kiss on her cheek and sauntered away.

Looking up, she saw Roman studying her from where he stood in the kitchen, and she froze at his expression. Ignoring the touch of annoyance that tightened in her gut, she nodded a good morning to him before heading up to her room. If they were going off on an adventure, Avery wanted to be prepared – not fumbling about and fawning over a man. Pushing Roman from her mind, she raced into her bedroom and dumped the granola bars on her bed. Going to the closet, she pulled out her emergency provision suitcase.

"Girl, what are you doing? You think we're packing for a wilderness safari?" Cherylynn put her hands on her hips and studied Avery, who had dropped to her knees and was digging through her bag.

"I like to be prepared. Notice they didn't say luxury yacht or spa day. They said adventure. I'm just going to bring a few things that could be helpful."

"I mean, a first aid kit is smart. But mosquito netting? Is that a hammock?" Cherylynn laughed.

"You won't be laughing if you have to sleep on the ground tonight. I have an extra." Avery raised an eyebrow at Cherylynn when she snatched it from her hands.

"You're right, I'm wrong, and you're amazing," Cherylynn decided. "Let's see what we can both fit. Here I was so focused on outfits and makeup that I didn't even think we might be sleeping outside."

"We might not. But I'm on top of it, if we are."

"Have I told you that I think you're incredibly smart?"

"Probably, but you can tell me again."

"You're brilliant, Avery. I'm glad you're my friend."

"And I am glad you're mine. Now get your pack, I want to see if we can fit extra water in."

"You can't be serious – you think they won't give us water?"

"I'll bring a knife in case we have to crack open coconuts," Avery decided, missing Cherylynn's eyeroll behind her back.

Nevertheless, when the call came that it was time to leave, both women felt ready to tackle whatever Siren Island might throw at them.

CHAPTER 16

"It wouldn't be a trip to an island in the Caribbean without a treasure hunt," Jack said, standing by the pool.

The women were gathered on the deck around the pool, staring at Jack like he was insane. Aside from Cherylynn and Avery, most of the woman were wearing slinky dresses and sexy sandals. Avery had gone with performance-wear shorts that dried quickly, a loose tank top, and a sun shirt that was tied around her waist. Completing her look was a broad-brimmed straw sunhat, her backpack, and Teva sandals that were easy to walk in, both in and out of the water. She watched as realization dawned on the women's faces and they glanced down at themselves. "You must divide into three teams immediately."

Lisette, Cherylynn, Avery, and Sara, the carpenter from the last challenge, all nudged closer together and sent nods to each other. Avery wasn't entirely sure what skills Lisette would bring to the table, but despite her outwardly ditsy vibe, Avery had found the woman to be fairly easygoing.

"Now that you have your teams, you'll each receive a map and set off on your treasure hunt at once. Beckett will join each team in turn as you head out on your journey. Best of luck!" Jack smiled his blindingly white smile at them. Avery imagined he would be kicking it poolside with a martini about five minutes after they left the villa.

One girl, in a sequined beach coverup, raised her hand to ask, "Can we just have a moment to return to our rooms quickly?"

"I'm sorry, but that isn't an option. Your challenge starts now," Jack said, and motioned for the women to head toward the beach where Beckett stood, maps in hand. The cameramen followed the group as the women glanced warily around and realized they just might not have properly prepared themselves for their task.

"Well, I don't think I'll be needing these," Lisette decided and quickly took off her platform sandals, tossing them beneath a nearby lounge chair.

"Are you okay to go barefoot?"

"Sure, no problem. I'm a California surfer girl. We run around barefoot all the time. I know I look high maintenance, but I can hack the elements," Lisette said, casually braiding her long sweep of hair and tying it off with a scrunchie she pulled from her wrist. Pulling a trucker-style hat from a woven bag slung over her shoulder, she tucked it on her head and smiled at the group.

"Perfect. What about you, Sara? Are you okay?" Avery studied the carpenter, noting that even though she wore a short fitted black dress, she also had a small bag on her shoulder.

"I'm fine. I can slip my flip-flops off if we're mucking through the water, and I brought a change of clothes, water, and sunscreen with me in my bag."

"I'd say we're more prepared than most. Let's saddle up and ride, ladies," Cherylynn said, a jaunty cowboy hat tucked on her head.

Beckett smiled at the group as they approached him, already lagging slightly behind the others, and held up the last map.

"I believe I have the key to your treasure, my ladies," Beckett said, his smile flashing white in his tanned face.

"And I have the key to your happiness," Lisette said smoothly, arching her back and preening for him. Beckett's grin widened as he took in Lisette's considerable assets before handing the map over to Sara without even looking at her. Sara rolled her eyes, and Avery bit back a grin, liking the woman more and more. It was nice to know that not every person here was fake or catty. Sleep had been difficult for her last night; she'd spent a lot of time thinking about comfort zones and what she was doing here. Avery missed talking to Ruby, who, despite her impulsive and headstrong nature, had always been a solid sounding board for her. She felt adrift here, Avery realized, and though she was doing her best to be involved in the game, it all felt so inauthentic to her. Was she just wasting her time?

"Care to take a peek, Avery?" Cherylynn asked, brandishing the map. Avery snapped out of her reverie, though she wished she'd had another cup of coffee, and moved closer to study the hand-drawn map. It was artfully aged to look like an old pirate map. Avery imagined some intern in an office spilling coffee on the paper and burning the edges to make it look worn and old. A rough outline of the island filled the page, with a large X marking a spot toward the south. In the bottom, there were clues written in what they must have thought was how pirates spoke.

"De treasure ye seek, she be beyond de peak. A siren's great sound, de bounty be found," Avery read, then flipped the page over to see if there was any other information.

"That's it?" Sara asked.

"That be all, matey," Cherylynn said, trying out a pirate impression.

"Yarr," Avery murmured, thinking back over her research of the island. "I think this is leading us to the south, where the cave and the siren statue are."

"Excuse me... what cave and siren statue? Did you already figure this out?" Cherylynn demanded, hands on her hips.

"Seriously? Did none of you read up on this island before you arrived?" Avery asked. She couldn't imagine being so blasé about traveling anywhere.

"I did," Sara admitted, leaning over the map. "And I do recall that there's either a siren statue, or some rocks that make a siren song at high tide or something. But I'm not certain I could lead you to them."

"I bet this one could," Cherylynn said, pointing at Avery. "First thing out of her mouth when we landed was talking about what side of the island we were on and trade winds and whatnot."

"Then we're lucky to have her on our team, aren't we?" Lisette smiled at Avery.

"South is that way. Best to follow the water," Avery said, checking the joke of a map once more before folding it up and putting it in her pack. It didn't surprise her in the least that they had been provided with as little information as possible. The standard operating procedure of these shows seemed to be setting people up for failure – apparently that was what made for good television.

"Ballpark on how long we're walking for?" Cherylynn asked, as they fell in line along the hardpacked sand just past the water's edge. A few cotton-ball style clouds dotted the sky, and a light breeze accompanied them on their walk.

"How long do you think these cameramen will walk for?" Sara wondered, nodding to where a cameraman walked ahead of them, catching all angles of their beach walk.

"I doubt for very long. But there's always a twist," Cherylynn said.

"Maybe they have cameramen set up on the next

leg," Lisette offered, tossing her braid behind her shoulder and pulling her coverup off to reveal a slinky turquoise bikini. "Might as well work on my tan." Avery admired the nonchalance with which she strutted her stuff, making the beach her catwalk. The cameramen were eating it up.

"Not a bad idea," Sara agreed, sliding out of her black coverup. Avery wondered if she'd been baking in the black, and was grateful for her own loose coverup. As nice as it might have been to slink along in her bathing suit, Avery just didn't have the skin for this sunlight. As the other women pulled clothes off, she donned her loose white sun shirt, buttoning it loosely so it covered her shoulders. If she remembered correctly, it was a long walk to the wall of cliffs where the siren rocks were located, and she'd be red as a lobster by day's end if she didn't protect herself now.

"I feel like the grandma of the bunch," Avery decided, laughing at herself. "I might as well have that white zinc paste on my nose."

"I think you look nice," Lisette said. "The loose button-down is its own kind of sexy look. Like it's begging to be unbuttoned and your hair let down. A lot of guys think that's sexy."

"You're really sweet, Lisette; thank you. I don't think I was thinking sexy when I pulled this on, so much as not frying to a little crisp like a vampire in sunlight."

"Work with what you got," Cherylynn shrugged. "We're all unique in our own way. And not any less beautiful for our differences."

"That's right. We're a team of badass babes and we're about to kick some treasure-hunting butts," Sara said. "Do we need a team name? What about a cheer?"

"Bountiful Beauties?" Cherylynn offered.

"Sassy Sirens?" Lisette asked.

"Savvy Sirens," Sara decided.

"I like it," Avery laughed, and brought her hand up for a team high-five. "Celebrating our looks and our brains. It's perfect." The women cheered and continued down the beach, chattering away in perfect accord.

Avery smiled, taking in the beautiful beach and her new friends. She found that despite her earlier misgivings about the fakeness of this show, she was actually having a good time. She doubted it would last – the catfights and drama would start again soon – but for now she was determined to take joy from this moment and pretend, for just a second, that she was a carefree adventurer having a wander down an unknown beach, just waiting to see what she'd discover.

She liked this Avery, and hoped she'd stick around.

CHAPTER 17

"They're losing their shit," Cherylynn whispered, peering around a cluster of bushes as one of the other groups descended into a full-on screaming match.

"I can hear," Lisette said, studying her nails before looking up at the group. "What should we do?"

"Watch them tear each other apart?" Cherylynn asked, her eyes alight with glee.

"I can go try to mediate," Avery offered, though she didn't think she was likely to make much headway. Especially now that one of the women was insulting the other's butt. She delivered the line well, but she lost points for meanness, Avery decided, peeking around the tree in time to see the woman with the aforementioned large butt tackle the other into the water. The cameras descended and madness ensued with a bevy of shrieks and insults.

"I think this is a good time to carry on and get ahead

of them," Sara decided. The group all looked at each other and nodded.

"Run for it?" Cherylynn whispered, pointing to a spot where the path along the beach narrowed between two cliff walls that came together like guards protecting a fortress.

"Go!" Avery agreed and together they dashed across the sand, not looking at the bedlam in the sand behind them – though Avery was pretty sure she saw a bikini top go flying into the air. Duly noted: Do not pick fights with these women, Avery thought. She gave a small shudder at the idea of brandishing her breasts on national television. A giggle bubbled up as she thought about it, and about the ridiculousness of them scrambling across the sand and ducking behind the cliff walls so the other group couldn't see them.

"I think we made it okay," Cherylynn said, fanning her face with her hand. "But we should keep moving on. How much longer you reckon, Avery?"

"Um…" Avery pulled out the poorly-drawn map and studied it, realizing it was really more of a cartoon than anything indicative of where they were. Relying on her memory, she looked around at the cliffs surrounding them. "I hate to say it, but it's either up the side of this cliff and over, or out in the water. And I'll be honest, I'm not going to handle going out in the water well."

"Why's that?" Beckett asked from behind her, causing her to jump what felt like a foot in the air.

"What the –! Beckett! Don't sneak up on people like

that," Avery gasped, bringing a hand to her chest. It felt like her heart was going to pop out of her skin.

"It's hardly 'sneaking up' with three cameramen and a producer lounging around," Beckett said, and Avery glanced around to see that the crew was hunkered down in the cavern they were in. They'd done a good job of concealing themselves, and she imagined it took some talent to blend into the background with a huge camera on your shoulder.

"Still. I swear you move like a panther," Avery grumbled, not enjoying being caught unawares but also not wanting to discuss her fear of water with Beckett.

"Wait until you see my other moves," Beckett said, his grin just shy of a leer.

Avery smacked him on the arm. "You'll have to work a lot harder for that," Avery promised. She turned away to scan the beach again, missing Beckett's approving gaze on her.

"I vote we climb as well. I don't like how the waves are crashing around those rocks." Cherylynn pointed. "See? It looks like there's some kind of current or undertow there, and I certainly don't need this pretty face getting smashed upside a rock, now, do I?"

"No, you do not," Beckett agreed. Cherylynn immediately shot him a sassy grin as he moved to her side. "I'd hate to see your perfection marred."

Cherylynn, true to her nature, whooped out a laugh and put her hand on Beckett's arm, gently squeezing his muscles.

"Honey, you're good for my ego, that's for damn

sure. I think I'll keep you around," Cherylynn said, laughing up at him. "Especially with these here strong muscles of yours. I can only imagine what kind of trouble they'd keep me out of."

Surely that wouldn't work on him, Avery thought, then rolled her eyes behind her sunglasses when Beckett flexed and the rest of the women dissolved into oohs and ahhs. Sometimes she wondered about the fragile male ego.

Avery left them behind to fawn over Beckett and made her way toward what looked like a small path leading through a pile of rocks and up toward the top of the cliff. Looking up, she gauged they'd have at least an hour or two hiking to the top, and who knew what lay on the other side. Glancing back out at the water that churned around the rocks at the base of the cliffs, Avery shuddered once more. This time her stomach did little flips as she thought about trying to swim out and around the rocks.

The funny thing was that she had once been a really strong swimmer. In fact, she likely still was – it wasn't a skill you just lost, Avery mused. She started the climb, knowing the other women would follow once they stopped drooling over Beckett. She'd grown up going to the lake on the weekends in the summer, spending hours in the water and jumping from the dock, or being pulled in a tube behind their motorboat. She'd only ever come in from the water when her mom would whistle for her to come inside; her dad would be standing by the grill, carefully attending to the meats he was cooking there.

Thinking of them made her smile – they'd had different reactions to her joining this show.

When she'd first told them, they'd both immediately asked if Ruby had put her up to it. Knowing their daughters well, it wasn't difficult to determine the root cause of Avery suddenly leaving her carefully cushioned existence for a wild trip to the Caribbean to film a reality television show. Her dad had been excited for her, happy to see her taking risks, and had started following all the blogs about the show online. He'd been the one to send her maps of the island and go over the history of where she was traveling to. Her mother, on the other hand, had been immediately worried for Avery. She'd been the one to stay with her for months after her accident, making her soup and helping her to feel normal again. Avery's mother knew better than anyone just what a huge step this trip was for her.

"Use good sense," her mother had cautioned. "And above all – be kind. You don't want to be one of those women who make other women look bad. We all need to support each other, not fight against each other. Women should lift other women up."

Thinking about her words, Avery turned back to make sure her group was still close behind her. They'd finally stopped fawning over Beckett and had now fallen in line on the hike, Beckett joining them. Avery turned back to the path. The sun's heat was relentless in the midday, and sweat trickled down her back beneath the pack she wore. Reaching for her water bottle, she took a swig and reminded herself to ration her sips, even though she'd likely get dehydrated. They really had no idea how long they'd be out here, and water was everything when it came to energy and survival in the heat like this. As the hours drew out, the group became silent, each lost in their own thoughts as they worked their way up the side of the cliff.

When they reached the apex, a generous breeze shot over the edge, bringing a smile of sweet relief to Avery's face. It had been exhausting to hike in the stillness all day, and now, at the top of the path, she welcomed the beautiful trade winds that the cliff wall had been blocking all day.

Her foot skidded and she forced herself to focus on where she was stepping. The path here was uneven, with loose gravel, bits of rock, and sand making the climb slippery. She had just turned to call out a warning about watching their steps when Sara shouted and went tumbling down the path.

"Sara!"

CHAPTER 18

"*I*s it broken?" Cherylynn hovered over Sara, who lay sprawled haphazardly across the path, her ankle twisted at an angle.

"I don't think so," Sara gasped, pushing herself up to a seated position. There was a swipe of dirt across her sweaty face and her eyes were wide. Gingerly, she wiggled her toes and moved her foot up and down. "But it's a nasty sprain, that's for sure. I've done this a few times now; I know the drill."

"We'll have to get you evacuated," Cherylynn said and looked directly at one of the cameramen. "Don't you have medical assistance?" The cameraman just shrugged and kept taping, and Avery's blood boiled.

"The incompetence of the producers running this show," Avery hissed, kneeling at Sara's side. "Listen, we're going to carry you to the top. There's a nice breeze, some shade behind some boulders, and I have a first aid kit with me. But you're looking a little shocky and I'd like to get you in the shade first before I deal with your ankle."

Sara nodded, her eyes wide, and Avery looked to Beckett.

"You'll have to carry her."

"I'm not sure I'm allowed..." Beckett trailed off as Avery stood up, hands on hips, and glared at him.

"You can and you will carry her to the top of this damn cliff because you're a decent human being. It doesn't matter what the rules are or if the cameras are running. She's hurt, and going into shock. Now pick her up and get your ass to the top of the cliff before I make you sorry you ever stepped foot on this stupid reality show."

"Yes, ma'am," Beckett said, his face flaming. He bent and scooped Sara easily into his arms.

"Watch that ankle," Avery warned, and raced ahead up the path until she found a spot in the shade. Dropping to her knees, she opened her pack and pulled out a thin quick-dry towel to lay on the ground, and her first aid kit. Motioning for Beckett to lay Sara on the towel, she instructed Cherylynn to come sit at her feet.

"Elevate her legs across yours," Avery instructed, and pulled out a travel ice pack. She cracked the crystals to activate the cold, and gently laid it over Sara's visibly swelling ankle. "Now, just let that cool there for a bit and we'll wait this out with you. It'll give you a moment while your adrenaline calms down a little." Avery sat next to Sara and held her hand, squeezing it while the woman breathed slowly, then looked up at Beckett, who hovered over them.

"You can't honestly think we're going to keep hiking like this, can you?"

"I... I don't know what happens in these circumstances. I'm sorry." Beckett held up his hands. "I can go ask. I'm sure Roman is lurking around here somewhere."

At Roman's name, Avery glanced wildly over her shoulder, trying to find him, but to no avail.

"You go find that man this instant, and you tell him that no show is worth someone's life. What if she falls and hurts herself more? What if the ankle is broken? This isn't a survival show. It's a dating show. I highly doubt she signed up for this. There has to be some sort of medical assistance," Avery fumed as she watched Beckett hike away.

"I can't imagine they would let her continue out here in the elements," Cherylynn agreed.

"Actually, they might," Lisette said, crouching on the other side of Sara's head and covering her with the coverup she'd pulled off earlier that day. Brushing her hair back, she felt Sara's forehead and made a small noise of distress. "It really depends on what Sara wants. Ultimately, I think she gets to make the decision."

"Is that true? No way," Avery said, her mouth open. She glanced back to the cliff that had just taken them hours to climb, and then out to where the sun dipped toward the horizon. It would be dark by the time they got to the bottom of the path again. There was no way

Sara would be able to maneuver or manage the path in darkness. She'd barely be able to do it in daylight, Avery thought, and frowned down at Sara's ankle while her brain whirled with various scenarios.

"I think I'm okay," Sara said, trying to sit up a bit, but Avery put a hand on her shoulder to push her back. "I'm not really in shock, I just get this rush to my head when I get injured. It's happened a few times on the job. At least I didn't faint this time."

"That's good. I don't need you going into full shock," Avery agreed, and glanced back at Sara's ankle propped on Cherylynn's leg. "But I do think your ankle is really hurt."

"It is. But it's not broken. Really. Do you have anything to wrap it with? I think if we wrap it and maybe find me a walking stick, I might be okay."

"Are you crazy? You don't want to make this any worse," Avery protested.

"I mean, what's my choice here? If they don't evacuate me, then I have to figure out a way down. Plus, I'm certain it's not as bad as it looks. I just get really really lightheaded when I hurt myself. I'm sure that made it look more dramatic than it is. Is there... can I have any water?"

Avery handed her the bottle from her pack and cautioned her to take small sips, then dug through the first aid kid for some anti-inflammatory pills.

"Take a few of these. I'm going to wrap it up now, if that's okay with you?" Avery asked, brandishing a roll of bandaging.

"Please. I'm sure I'll be fine. I don't want to go yet," Sara whispered.

Avery sighed, annoyed that people were more concerned with a stupid show than basic safety.

After Avery's accident, she'd become an emergency first responder, hoping to help manage some of the stress that lingered from that day. Her training took over as she carefully wrapped Sara's ankle, then she checked to see how many other ice packs she had with her.

"I'd like you to stay off this foot as best you can," Avery instructed. She looked up as Cherylynn drew her attention. "What?"

"The sun'll be setting in the next hour or so. I think we need to figure out shelter and some sort of crutches for her if we do plan to stay here. Otherwise it's going to be an uncomfortable, and dark, night out here."

"I have headlamps," Avery said, pulling two from her bag.

"I think I love you," Cherylynn decided.

"I am a little neurotic when it comes to being prepared," Avery admitted, then looked down at Sara. "Are you cool to chill here while we scope out the top of this cliff and figure out our plan for the night?"

"No problem." Sara smiled meekly. "I'm sorry I'm dragging you guys down. I should've watched my step better."

"Don't worry about it. We'll figure this out," Avery promised, and patted Sara's shoulder reassuringly.

"Okay, so what are we looking for exactly?" Lisette asked.

"Shelter for the night, maybe a way to make a fire, sticks or something we can fashion into a walking stick or crutches for Sara, and maybe – ideally – a way off this cliff. Maybe the other side isn't as bad," Avery said. The three girls stood, hands on hips, and turned in a slow circle surveying their surroundings. Avery glared at the camera guy who followed them, furious that he wasn't stepping in to help.

"Tamp down on that look, killer," Cherylynn whispered as they took off toward the edge of the cliff.

"It's just absolutely infuriating to me. She needs help – people should help her. I don't understand how this is even a question," Avery bit out.

"It makes for good TV. My guess is that if she was really seriously hurt they'd come and get her."

"I should hope so. I don't think watching someone die on television is exactly thrilling." Avery rolled her eyes as they came to the edge of the cliff. Together, the three of them surveyed what lay on the other side.

"Wow... this is insane," Lisette said, looking down at the expanse of private beach that beckoned to them from below. Beautiful white sand was sheltered by rock walls and a long line of palm trees. It looked restful, calm, and inviting. Turning, Avery studied the top of the cliff they now stood on. Aside from the pile of boulders that Sara sat propped against, there was nothing but jagged rocks and a few small, stubby cactus plants surrounding them. Here, they'd be exposed to the elements – wind, rain, and sun. If they could get down to the beach, they'd have more protection.

"Do you think we can make it down there?" Chery-lynn asked.

"Look, the path is over here. It actually looks way more gentle than the way we came up. See? It sort of slopes down the side of the cliff and switches back. I bet Sara could do that much more easily than the other way we came."

"What happens once we're down there, though?" Avery demanded.

"Well… look." Cherylynn pointed to where the beach wrapped around the other side of the cove. "You can walk on the smooth sand over there. And I bet there's something on the other side, isn't there? I swear I can see lights."

"There should be another village on that side," Avery agreed, going over her mental map of the island. "We were smack in the middle of the east coast, and there are definitely more developments on the south end."

"So, if we get her down and around that beach in the morning, I bet we can flag down a car or help. Plus, the treasure might be in this little spot here, right? Weren't the cliffs where the sirens sang or something? If we get Sara down, find the treasure, and get her out safely – we all win!" Cherylynn smiled brightly at Avery.

"That's a lot of 'if's.'"

"Got a better plan?" Cherylynn asked, her voice sweet as honey.

"No, I really don't. I don't think we'll be comfort-able up here on this rock tonight," Avery admitted.

"Hey, there's some driftwood here," Lisette called from the other side of the ledge, brandishing a gnarled stick. "I think someone had a bonfire up here at some point."

"There's our crutches," Cherylynn said.

Avery sighed, running her palm over her face. "Fine, let's do this. But I'd like to go on record as stating that I think the producers should medically evacuate someone who is hurt," Avery said, raising her voice and looking around just in case Roman was lurking nearby.

"It's on the record. Stamped and sealed. Now, come on, let's go make some crutches."

"You know, I could be home with a good book right now," Avery grumbled.

"And I could be shopping the fall sale at Nordstrom. Nevertheless, here we both are. Let's build us some shelter and watch a beautiful sunset."

"If we get to the bottom in time," Avery said, stooping to gather as many of the driftwood sticks as she could.

"We will, we will," Lisette promised. Together they took every last bit of driftwood they could find and brought it over to Sara, piling it in front of her.

"Well, you guys get an A+ for gathering skills," Sara decided, smiling up at them. "If you have any rope, or even a knife, I can build a crutch."

"Well, let's see this crutch you keep talking about. If you can even build it?" Lisette demanded.

"Carpenter, remember? I just need to create a notch for the pieces and I should be okay."

"Knife," Avery said, handing Sara a serviceable Swiss Army knife from her pack.

"Perfect. Let me get to work. Tell me what I'm dealing with to get off this cliff," Sara said. Cherylynn filled her in on their plan as she picked up stick after stick and discarded them. When she found one that seemed to measure about to her shoulder, she set it aside and picked out two smaller pieces.

When she was done, Avery carefully bundled the rest of the wood and tied it with a climbing rope she had in her pack.

"A true survivalist," Lisette said. "You have rope, a knife, a first aid kit... how did you know to pack all this?"

"I don't particularly like being caught off guard. In fact, when I first found out I was coming here, I kept thinking we'd be sleeping on the beach and building our own huts. I wasn't really expecting a luxurious villa. So I packed all this stuff. It was my... friend who made me pack all my different outfits."

"Looks like your premonition is coming true – we *are* going to be sleeping on the beach and building our own shelter. So, I guess, good job on being prepared. I'm really glad I partnered with you."

"Thanks, Lisette. Think you can carry this stack down?" Avery motioned to one of the bundles of sticks.

"No problem. I'm here to be your pack mule."

"How are your feet holding up?" Avery asked, realizing suddenly that Lisette had been barefoot this whole time.

"Scratched, a little sore, but nothing I can't handle. Don't worry, you won't have to carry me out of here."

"Roman and Beckett will have to be carried out of here after I'm done with them," Avery promised, hoisting her bundle of driftwood and attaching it to the back of her pack.

Cherylynn stood, helping Sara to her feet. She had made a nice-looking crutch from what, moments before, had been scraps of driftwood. Avery held her breath as Sara took a few wobbly steps forward and then got the hang of it.

"I'm good! Let's keep going, ladies," Sara said. "I have a feeling we'll find this treasure down there."

"Shall we?" Lisette said, looking at Avery, who seemed to have become the de facto leader of this little group.

"I don't think we have a choice."

"Saddle up," Cherylynn cried.

"Do you think she says that every morning as she starts her day?" Lisette wondered.

Avery burst out laughing, watching as Cherylynn hovered close to Sara, ready to catch her if she fell.

"I'm certain. Her daddy's a rancher, after all."

"That explains so much."

CHAPTER 19

*M*aybe she had overreacted, Avery thought, second-guessing herself on the way down from the top of the cliff. There was something about trauma and injury out in the wild that dredged up remnants of pain from her own experience in the rapids. It might not make sense, but then nobody ever said that emotions were rational. She had every right to feel the way she did, Avery reminded herself – or so her therapist had said. She was supposed to honor those feelings, and understand that she was still dealing with the ramifications of almost dying.

Mainly, she just felt angry. More specifically, angry at Roman. For some reason, even though the man seemed to make the hairs on the back of her neck prickle, she had thought more highly of him. Yet he'd disappointed her today, she realized. She wasn't sure if she'd been expecting a knight in shining armor to save Sara, but at the very least, a competent medical professional on the scene would have been nice. Instead, she'd had to be her own hero.

And wasn't that a revelation? Avery skidded to a stop, as the women continued down the path. She took a deep breath, and then another. Her gaze took in the view – the way the sun was kissing the water, the frigatebird that swooped lazily overhead, and how the leaves of the palms fluttered together in the breeze. Here she was, on a random island in the Caribbean, exposing herself to national television, and she hadn't broken or failed when her friend got hurt far away from help. Instead, she'd handled it like a boss, and now they were on their way to making a shelter and settling in for the night. Everyone was safe, nobody was going to die, and that was in large part due to her actions.

A newfound sense of power filled Avery, its warmth coursing through her core, as she realized that maybe she didn't need to be chained so much to the fears of the past. She could be her own hero. It was time for her to stop living small and start embracing life again – in all its ups and downs. That was what Ruby had been trying to tell her for years now, she realized, and the source of the worry that hovered in her parents' eyes when they looked at her. She'd cocooned herself in a ball of virtual cotton wool, keeping herself as sheltered and safe as she could. But was that really how she wanted to live her life?

"You gonna give a speech or something?" Chery-lynn called from below. The other three had made it to the beach, and Avery realized she was still standing halfway up the path, looking out over the beach.

"I could, but I don't want to bore you," Avery laughed, and all but scampered the rest of the way down the path, feeling happier than she had in years. It was as though virtual chains around her shoulders had snapped, and a lightness filled her being.

"Well? What say you, O fearless leader?" Cherylynn asked, saluting as Avery neared the group.

"Sara? How much pain are you in?"

"Manageable," Sara said, rotating her ankle slightly. "Though if you have another ice pack, I'll take it. Or maybe I can submerge my foot in the water to cool it a little bit."

"I do have two more ice packs I can activate. Can you wait just a bit while we find a spot and then we'll settle in?"

"No problem. Over there looks nice." Sara pointed to a small cluster of palms on the side of the beach, sheltered by the rock wall. "There's shade from the trees, but it's still sandy beach, so it'll be soft to sit on."

"That looks good. Let's go set up what we can, then we'll get some ice on you," Avery said, glaring again at the cameraman who hovered nearby. Just because she could be her own hero didn't mean she wasn't annoyed at the lack of medical assistance from the crew.

"I wonder what happened to Beckett," Lisette said when they got to the cluster of palms and dropped their packs on the ground. Avery unhooked the bundle of sticks and set them in the sand, then opened her pack.

"Too much hard work so he ran away?" Avery said. She pulled the hammocks from her pack, then untied the rope from the bundle of sticks.

"Geez, Avery," Sara laughed. "You told him to go."

"Well? He should be back by now. I didn't mean leave us out here alone. What kind of man runs when you've hurt yourself? Is that really what you want in a partner?" Avery wondered.

"I thought he was running for help," Sara said.

"Is he though? I mean, there are cameramen here. All of whom have walkie-talkies clipped to their belts, and likely cell phones as well. I don't doubt that any one of them could have radioed for help and you would have been evacuated by now."

"True," Sara said. She sighed. "Well, everyone has their faults."

Avery thought it showed his true character and was more than a fault, but she kept her words to herself. Instead, she busied herself with tying the two hammocks between the trees. Standing back, she surveyed her work and nodded. Now she just had to figure out two more beds.

"Sara, would you like my hammock?" Cherylynn asked.

"I… no, I couldn't possibly," Sara said, a frown deepening her pretty face. "I've already caused too much trouble."

"It's really not a problem. I've slept on the ground more times than I can count. When we ride the ranch – which is thousands of acres, mind you – I've had to sleep in a bedroll on the ground. This sand is nice and cushy compared to that."

"I'm happy to sleep on the beach too." Lisette shrugged. "I've napped in the sand a ton between surf sessions. It's no bother to me."

"You're sure?" Sara asked.

"No problem. I can use my pack as a pillow," Lisette promised, patting Sara's shoulder.

"Should I start building a fire?" Cherylynn asked. The sun had fallen below the horizon and a brilliant display of red and orange streaks lingered in the sky.

"I think that'll be good. It'll help keep bugs away. Here's my bug repellent, too." Avery handed over the bottle.

"Seriously, how much stuff do you have in that pack?" Sara wondered out loud. She hobbled over to a hammock, lowering herself gently while the group collectively held their breath, then sighed in relief when she didn't flip back out the other side.

"More pills, if you're in pain," Avery said, shaking the bottle at her.

"I'll take some in a bit. I'm okay for now. I don't know how long we'll be out here, so I'd like to ration them."

"Speaking of rations," Cherylynn chimed in. She had made a neat teepee of sticks in a hole she'd dug in the sand and surrounded it with a circle of rocks. "What's our water situation looking like?"

"I have one full bottle," Lisette said.

"I have half a bottle," Sara said.

"I have almost a full bottle, half a bottle, and a water purifying mechanism," Avery said. She paused when the rest just looked at her.

"You brought a water purifier?"

"Yeah, you just pour it through and let it do its thing. It's meant for travel. And I have back-up purifying tablets." Avery looked around at them. "What?"

"I feel like you were a Girl Scout," Lisette decided.

"I might have been." Avery shrugged. "Oh, and I have about fifteen granola bars, so it might not be the most exciting dinner, but it's something."

"Oh, thank god. I was not about to catch a fish and cook it," Lisette said.

"If you want to, though, I can filet them. I used to fish a lot," Sara offered.

"I think I'm good with the granola bars," Avery said, eying the dark water warily. She hadn't thought to bring a fishing line or a hook, though in retrospect that wouldn't have made sense. Like she'd know the first thing about how to catch a fish or cut it up and cook it.

"Please tell me you have matches? I'm not ready to rub two sticks together for an hour, though I can if I have to." Cherylynn eyed Avery hopefully.

"Even better – a waterproof lighter." Avery dug around until she found the lighter. Pulling out another ice pack, she activated it as she walked over to Sara's hammock, and handed it to her. "I'm going to just wander around the cove here, maybe find a spot for a toilet away from the cameraman."

"You could just go pee in the water. That's what I'm going to do," Lisette offered.

"I am not wading into dark water at night."

"I'm sure it's fine."

"Nope. Enjoy your creepy death-water pee. I'm going to hide behind a bush," Avery said. She switched her headlight on; then, seeing one of the cameramen move as if to follow her, she stopped and looked directly at the camera.

"I'm going to pee. You do not have permission to follow me." The cameraman flashed her a grin and nodded, swinging back to where the other girls sat as the first lick of flames climbed up the pile of driftwood.

Happy she'd held her ground, Avery followed the line of the cliff wall until she found a secluded spot behind a bush, and took care of her business. On the walk back, she stopped, her eyes caught by something glinting out in the water near a cluster of rocks. For a moment, she could've sworn a fish – or something – had jumped from the water. She wondered if those were the siren rocks she'd read about; from here, with the last rays of light caressing the sky, they did look somewhat like a siren rising from the sea.

"Guys, I think we're close to the treasure," Avery said, bounding back to the others. "Look out at those rocks. What do you think?"

"I... guess they kind of look like a siren. But aren't they supposed to make noises? Like a song?"

"At high tide, I think," Avery said.

"What is it now?"

"I don't know if it is just coming in or going out, but it looks mid-way," Lisette offered.

"And since I don't hear any rocks singing away, I'm guessing it's not high tide, honey," Cherylynn said.

"Should we try to get out to them?"

"In the dark?" Avery asked.

"Well, if the tide's low and the treasure's out there – wouldn't that make sense?" Lisette asked.

"I... damn it, yes, it makes sense. If – and that's a big if – these are the rocks, and the treasure is there, then yes, getting to them at low tide would be smart." Avery couldn't believe she was actually agreeing to this.

"Then we go," Cherylynn decided.

"You could wait until morning," Sara said.

"We need to get you out of here in the morning, not be spending time treasure-hunting," Avery said.

"Besides, if the other groups get here in the night and they take the treasure, then we lose," Lisette said.

"What are we winning, anyway?" Avery wondered.

"Likely we'll automatically progress to the next round," Lisette said.

"It would be a lot cooler if it was money," Cherylynn grumbled, standing up and wiping the sand from the back of her legs.

"I can't believe I'm agreeing to do this," Avery said. "But – let's go find that treasure."

"Go get 'em, girl," Sara said, swinging herself to a sitting position in the hammock, her legs hanging over the side. "I'll keep the fire stoked while you're gone."

"Great, thank you," Avery said.

"Don't do anything stupid," Sara warned. "I've already handicapped us."

"I don't think there's anything bright about what we're doing, so we've already lost there," Avery muttered as they plodded along the water's edge to where the line of rocks stretched far into the sea.

"It's an adventure," Cherylynn reminded her.

"Aye, matey, let's find our gold doubloons," Avery tried out, then added a "Yarr" for good measure.

"You'll need to work on that," Cherylynn decided.

CHAPTER 20

On the list of stupid things she'd done in her life – which honestly wasn't that long if you didn't count the stunts that Ruby pulled her into periodically – this had to be pretty high up there, Avery decided as they climbed over rocks slick with algae and covered with barnacles. Night had settled upon them and only the light from the two headlamps and the rising moon showed their path. They moved slowly, Cherylynn in the front with her light, Lisette in the middle with no light, and Avery in the back, lighting the way for both Lisette and herself as they did their best not to slip and slide across the rocks or get sliced by the sharp shells of the barnacles.

Lisette moved with ease and confidence, her bare feet hugging the rocks, and Avery could see more and more clearly that she was an ocean-going California girl. Nothing really seemed to gross her out or bother her, which was not what Avery would have expected when she first met her. She'd assumed that Lisette would be the first to scream at a bug or cry at a broken nail, yet she'd done nothing but be kind, easy-going, and funny to be around this whole time. It wouldn't be hard for Beckett to fall in love with someone like her, Avery thought as they clambered over a particularly large boulder. The waves snapped against the rocks, slapping saltwater in their faces, and Avery paused to wipe her eyes so she could see again.

She herself, on the other hand, seemed to be a bit of a mess, she realized. Even though she'd had a nice epiphany on the beach earlier, it had been kind of like ripping the Band-Aid off, and now all sorts of emotions were flooding through her. The realization that she'd essentially become a hermit to protect herself was making her sad for the years she'd lost, not to mention the bitterness about men she'd also managed to pick up along the way.

It had hurt, more than she'd admitted to anyone, when her boyfriend had left her after the accident. He hadn't signed up to help someone recover from such a catastrophic event, and had left her with a "Glad you're not dead" shortly after she'd come out of the coma. Sure, they'd only been dating for six months, but Avery had expected he would stay by her side through a tough situation. The harsh reality of recovery mixed with rejection had spiraled her into a pretty low point in her life. Could anyone blame her for not trusting men after that?

"What are you muttering about back there?" Lisette

asked as they continued to climb over the rocks, the light of the fire growing smaller by the second. Avery wondered if or how the cameramen were catching this – she couldn't imagine that they would be climbing over these boulders with cameras on their shoulders.

"Um, just… nothing, really," Avery said, pushing her stuff to the side to focus on the task at hand.

"Come on, give it up," Cherylynn said.

"I… I had a bad accident a few years back. In the water. I don't like talking about it, but it makes me leery of being this close to the ocean."

"Can you not swim?" Lisette stopped and looked back at her, genuine concern on her pretty face.

"No, I'm a great swimmer. It was a kayak-and-fast-rapids kind of accident. Again, nothing I really like to revisit. Just left some marks on me, I guess."

"Well, yeah, duh. That sounds really scary. Were you hurt badly?"

"I was in a coma for a week," Avery said before she could shut herself up. She'd promised herself she wouldn't share this, as she didn't want a pity party. When she'd been recovering from the accident, there had been nothing she'd hated more than people giving her those kind of looks when she was slowly getting up strength to walk again and so on. The last thing she wanted was to be treated with kid gloves in this competition.

"Holy shit, I'd say that's a big deal," Cherylynn said, shooting a look over her shoulder, though all Avery could see was the blinding light of her headlamp.

"Headlamp," Avery laughed, throwing her hand in front of her eyes.

"Oh yeah, sorry." Cherylynn looked down quickly. "But for real – how scary. And here you are crawling on these rocks with us. I'd say that takes some major cojones, girl."

"I don't get why guys get the credit for being strong," Lisette complained. "Balls have to be, like, the weakest thing ever. Seriously, have you seen a guy get kicked in the sack before? Or hit accidently with something there? It's like the world literally ends, I swear, the screaming and carrying-on they do. Rolling around on the floor like someone just threw acid on their face or something. Balls aren't strong. Women should get the credit for being strong. We're the ones who can push ten-pound footballs out of us and get up and walk the same day. Now you tell me what's stronger? Balls or vajayjays?" Lisette demanded. She seemed to suddenly realize that the other two women had stopped walking to stare at her as she ranted.

"Well, shit, you're right," Cherylynn decided.

"Of course I'm right. Women are strong and amazing and all-powerful. So, yes, Avery, you've got some major vajayjay power to be out here climbing on the rocks with all this dark water swirling around you."

If someone had ever told Avery that one day she'd laugh until she cried while perched on a boulder far from shore with dark water teeming at her feet, she would have called them a liar.

"Oh my gosh! X marks the spot! X marks the spot!"

Cherylynn shrieked. Sara cheered from the beach, and they all turned. The fire looked impossibly far away, and Avery gulped at the dread that rushed through her. She forced herself to draw on this newfound strength inside her.

Turning back, she quickly clambered over the last boulder, ignoring the twist in her gut when her foot slipped a bit, and peered over Lisette's shoulder. She did her best to ignore the water circling her feet, trying not to think too deeply about what was swimming around in there, and laughed when she saw what Cherylynn had found.

Tied to a trio of three rocks – which, up close, did look strikingly like the form of a woman or a seal, head thrown upwards and back arched – was a large X made out of driftwood sticks, with a silver pouch duct-taped to the middle.

"I wonder who got the job of bringing this out here," Lisette said.

"I was just thinking that. Likely the same intern who made that crappy map," Cherylynn decided. "Avery, you didn't bring that knife, did you?"

"In my pocket," Avery said, and handed it over.

Cherylynn neatly cut the pouch away and tucked it inside her swim top for safe keeping. "I don't know about you," she said, "but I'm more than ready to get back to shore before this water gets any higher. Anyone else notice it creeping up our legs?"

Now that Cherylynn had mentioned it, Avery did notice the crash of waves getting louder. Panic loomed in her throat, and she put a hand to her chest, struggling to catch her breath.

"Now you just go on and breathe, honey. There's nothing to it but one foot in front of the other all the way back to shore," Cherylynn said, ignoring a particularly large wave that slammed at their knees. "Slow and steady. It's when you rush that you slip up."

"She's right," Lisette said, turning Avery firmly around and nudging her back toward shore. "Steady as she goes. We have plenty of time. High tide doesn't just rush into shore in five minutes. We'll be back on that beach long before these rocks are covered in water."

"Okay, got it," Avery said, breathing in through her nose and out through her mouth. She forced down the panic that licked at her stomach. "Go slow, Avery, go slow, Avery." She chanted it to herself the whole way back to shore, focusing on the words and her steps, whispering it like a mantra over and over until once again her feet touched sand. Had she been a more dramatic person, she would have dropped to her knees and cast her arms to the stars, praising whatever universal energy was out there for seeing her safely back. Instead she turned and hugged her friends.

"Thank you for your help," she said. "I'm sorry I had a moment out there."

"Honey, if you call that a moment, then I don't know what we'd call it when *I* have a moment. A tornado?"

"A tantrum?" Lisette suggested.

"A tsunami?" Cherylynn said.

"A car crash?" Avery said. They all laughed,

hooking arms and running back down the beach, excited to show Sara what they'd found. She stood by the fire, the crutch under one arm, and added more wood.

"I am so glad you all are back," Sara admitted. "I have to admit, you looked really far away out there. I didn't like thinking you might slip and hit your head or something." Then she whooped when Cherylynn pulled the pouch from her top. "You found it!"

"We're okay. It was tricky, I'm not going to lie," Avery said, plopping down on the sarongs that Sara had laid out next to the fire. "But we did manage."

"Boy, am I glad we're back, though," Cherylynn said. "I just wish we had some wine."

"Well..." Avery said.

The whole group turned with their mouths open in shock.

"Please tell me you didn't carry heavy bottles with you in your pack," Sara demanded.

"Or please tell me you did?" Cherylynn asked hopefully.

"Not bottles. I took the bag out of a box of wine they had in the kitchen and shoved it in my pack last minute. Just in case." Avery laughed and dug the bag of red wine from the bottom of her pack.

"You are officially my new favorite person," Cherylynn decided.

"Let's see what's in the bag," Avery said, blushing at their compliments. Opening the wine, she took a drink from the nozzle, and then handed it out. As the ladies passed the wine around the circle, Avery began handing out power bars for dinner.

"Sara, you open it." Cherylynn handed it off.

"No, I shouldn't," Sara said, guilt crossing her face.

"Open it. We're a team," Lisette insisted, taking another swig of the wine before passing it back to Avery.

"Ohhh, gold coins." Sara giggled and held up four fake gold coins. "They say, 'Automatically advance to the next round.'"

"Sweet! I feel like I just got one of those extra life mushrooms in the Mario games." Cherylynn laughed. "Cheers, ladies! I know it's going to be a long night, but hopefully nothing else eventful will happen and we can get out safely in the morning."

A haunting, ethereal howling rang across the water, and the women froze, eyes huge in their faces, as the sound continued. It wasn't quite a song – as there was no rhythm or melody to it – but it still tugged at Avery's heart. In its own way, it was beautiful.

"It's the rocks... the siren rocks," Lisette said, looking out to where they'd just been.

"They're singing for us," Avery said, happy to have been back on land and not near the rocks when they'd started up. She could see now why they warned sailors away from the rocks – as the water came in, the rocks were barely visible.

"It's incredible," Cherylynn decided.

"I'll always remember this moment," Avery said. "Cheers, ladies. Thank you for sharing this with me."

CHAPTER 21

*A*very wasn't sure what woke her or, frankly, where she was for a moment. She blinked up at the palm leaves fluttering over her head and took a few seconds to calibrate her brain. Turning her head, she saw Cherylynn and Lisette, both comfortably sleeping by the fire that had died down to just embers. Sara snored in her hammock, and the moon had risen high enough that its light illuminated the beach.

They'd finished most of the wine, which was likely the reason the other women were sleeping so comfortably right now. Avery had drunk far less than they had. She'd never been one to hold her liquor well, so typically two glasses of wine was more than enough for her. She didn't like the feeling of being out of control that came from too many drinks, instead enjoying the light buzz she got from just one or two glasses. The rest of the women had no problem with wine, and had indulged themselves while telling stories about their past boyfriends that made Avery laugh so hard she'd had to go use her toilet bush again. All in all, it had been a fun and successful evening, and the camaraderie they'd built together was something that would warm Avery's heart for a long time to come.

The sound pulled her head up once again, and Avery squinted out at the ocean. Were the rocks singing again? It sounded different this time, she realized, much more melodic. If she'd been a betting woman, she would have put money down that there was a woman out in the water, singing her very heart out.

Desperate to see what was creating such a hauntingly beautiful song, Avery slipped from her hammock and crept toward the shore, leaving the sleeping women behind. As she approached the water, the song grew louder, and it began to wrap around her, seducing her gently with its notes. She didn't realize she was crying until a tear ran down her cheek and plopped onto her hand.

What sorrow hung in those notes, Avery thought, her heart aching in her chest. She found herself running down the beach, desperate to help this woman singing of love and loss. The words were indecipherable, a language unknown to Avery, but the melody translated everything she needed to know. She was dying of a broken heart, whoever she was, and Avery needed to help her.

"There she is," Avery whispered. She froze, not even realizing that she was already waist deep in the water. A woman rose from the sea, far out in the deep.

This wasn't a normal woman – oh no; she was an ethereal being, a goddess of the sea, her hair slicked wet in coils around her head, her skin alabaster white and glowing in the light of the moon that bathed her.

Her eyes locked on Avery and for a moment, Avery felt like someone had shot a million beams of light into her very soul. Then the woman dove into the water, brandishing a tail that flashed a rainbow of colors, and the song died with her disappearance.

"No," Avery gasped, going deeper into the water. "Please don't go. Don't be sad. I'll help you. Whatever you need, I can help you."

"What do you think you're doing?" A hand grasped her arm and wrenched Avery back, plastering her against a very wet, very muscular, and very angry Roman.

"I... I..." Avery threw a glance over her shoulder back out at the dark waves, where the line of light from the moon shimmered in a path across the sea, and then down at where she stood, almost up to her neck in the dark water, and then up at Roman.

"Are you insane? Do you think you can just walk into the dark water at night? All alone? Far away from help? I should throttle you," Roman bit out, his face thunderous, her body still pressed tightly against him. She squirmed, but he held her caged against him as he regulated his breathing.

"Did you see?" Avery gasped, looking once more back to the sea, a torrent of emotions racing through her. Shock raged with lust as her body began to respond instinctively to being pressed against Roman's muscular body, and she wondered when the last time was she'd been held by a man.

"I saw you being an absolute fool and wandering into the water. Was I not clear on the rules?" Roman asked, his grip loosening a bit, and Avery eased back, realizing that his anger was a mask for fear.

"I'm sorry. I have no idea what came over me – but did you see?" Avery asked, looking back out over the water. As long as she lived, she knew, she would never forget that moment.

"See what? Just how much did you have to drink tonight?"

Avery narrowed her eyes at him, anger quickly surging over the torrent of other emotions that knotted her stomach. A part of her wanted nothing more than to drag Roman's lips down to hers and kiss him with all the longing and abandon that the siren's song demanded, and a part of her wanted to shove her fist into his gut for leaving them out here and insinuating she was stupid enough to drink and jump in the water.

"I barely had anything to drink. I'm not a big drinker, which is why I'm not currently passed out in the sand," Avery hissed, stabbing a finger into his chest. He grabbed her hand and pulled her with him, hauling her out of the water. Finally they stood back on the moonlit sand, both of them dripping wet, Avery gasping for air.

"Then what the hell were you doing?"

"Didn't you hear? The song? And – wait just a

minute. Where did you come from, anyway?" Avery demanded, her hands on her hips. "I've been wondering where you were all day. Sara's hurt and you idiots have done nothing to help her."

"I'm aware she is hurt," Roman said, crossing his arms over his chest and staring down at her. Why did he make her want to nuzzle into him and lick her way down his body?

And just where had *that* thought come from?

"Wow, great job you're doing on looking out for your people, then." Avery rolled her eyes.

"I got here as soon as I could. And from what I can tell, you handled it just fine. There's nothing to be done at three in the morning anyway, so I figured sleep would be the best thing for everyone – especially considering how much wine she had. It wouldn't do to try and take a tipsy, injured woman out of here. She'd probably just end up hurting herself more."

The man had a point, though Avery refused to acknowledge it.

"It's three in the morning. It was broad daylight when she was injured. She could have been hurt even worse going down the side of the cliff. Beckett supposedly went to find you for help. And don't tell me your cameramen didn't radio you that there was an injury. What could possibly have taken you this long to show up?"

"Oh, so you think you're the only one on this show? That Sara is the only one who got injured today? The only one who had to go to the hospital today? I'm one person, Avery. I had to assess who needed my help most."

Avery paused at that and looked closer at his face to see a very real fatigue etched on his handsome features.

"Someone else got hurt?"

"Yes, someone else got hurt. And hurt each other. Two of the women got into a fistfight and one broke the other's nose. Another got hit by a stingray and had an allergic reaction. I'm sorry I wasn't here in the timely manner that you expected, but I had to deal with the worst emergencies first. I'm here now, though, and I have to say I'm glad I arrived when I did. Just what the hell were you doing out in the water like that?"

"I... I don't know. I'm sorry, Roman. I shouldn't have bitten your head off. I've been angry all day that nobody helped Sara."

"*You* helped Sara. You followed all the proper protocols, from what I heard. The crew was keeping me updated, and you did everything right. We'll get her out of here in the morning, and she'll be just fine."

"Thank you," Avery whispered, feeling that strength flood her once more. "I was scared for her, is all."

"And you handled it. You should be proud of yourself. But this... I don't know what this was. You about gave me a heart attack, walking into the water in a trance like that. Don't... just don't do that, okay?" Roman's eyes searched hers.

Once more Avery realized that she wanted nothing more than to kiss him. Tilting her head up, she leaned in a little, the moment drawing out long between them.

"I heard the siren's song," Avery whispered. "Have you heard it? It's enchanting."

Roman's eyes dropped to Avery's lips and lingered there. He licked his own lips, and Avery felt heat rush through her stomach. Just an inch closer and they'd be kissing.

"I've heard it... I swear you're a siren yourself, Avery. I can't stop watching you," Roman whispered. Reaching up, he trailed a finger down her arm, the smallest touch sending shivers through her body.

"Avery! Are you okay?" Cherylynn called, her voice breaking the stillness.

Avery shook her head, stepping back from Roman and making her way around him. She could see Cherylynn on the beach, looking around wildly, as the other girls woke up in shock. Glancing over her shoulder at Roman, the moment broken, she watched as he faded back into the darkness.

"Go to them."

"Cherylynn, I'm here. It's okay. I was just stopping at my toilet bush," Avery called. She mentally kicked herself for saying 'toilet bush' in front of Roman and hurried back to the other women, her stomach in knots.

If someone had told her it was all a dream, she would have believed it.

Avery smiled brightly at Cherylynn.

"Why are you all wet?"

"I got some pee on my leg. Now shhhh, go back to sleep."

CHAPTER 22

$\mathcal{R}$oman had heard the song – of course he'd heard it. It was as though the notes were being sung for him and him alone. In all his time traveling the world, exploring the depths of jungles or forests, nothing had ever ripped into his gut and taken him to his knees the way that song had. He wondered how the other women and his cameramen hadn't heard it – was it possible they *couldn't* hear it? Was he slowly going crazy?

Avery had heard it. When he'd seen her walk into the water, his heart had skipped a beat and he'd been after her before he could think. Never mind the fact that his phone was in his pocket or that a part of him wanted to swim with Avery, slicing through the dark water together until they found the source of such magic and beauty. Instead, he'd hauled her back against him like a Neanderthal and almost taken her head off. If he hadn't been so scared for her, or already at the end of his emotional tether, maybe he would have been gentler. Instead, he'd wrenched her from the water and yelled at her.

And then told her how he couldn't help watching her.

Groaning, Roman slapped a hand to his face and shook his head. Where had that little tidbit come from? He was usually in control when it came to his relationships with women. He liked to keep things respectful, but distant. His work took him away on so many travels that it was hard to form deeper bonds. As far as he was concerned, so long as he was up front and honest about his intentions, his lifestyle, and his travels, nobody got hurt. There were plenty of women in his life who were more than happy to have a casual friends-with-benefits style relationship, enjoying each other when he was in town but no commitments when he left. It suited him, and his lifestyle, perfectly.

Had he hurt feelings along the way? Roman stretched his legs out on the bedroll he'd laid out behind a row of boulders tucked near the cliff walls. His crew members slept on, used to weird sleeping conditions; all of them were able to fall asleep pretty much anywhere at this point. Yes, Roman thought, he'd hurt a few feelings over the years. But not because of lying or being untruthful, Roman reminded himself. It was because he'd dated women who thought they would change him.

How many times had he needed to remind a woman that his life was full of travel? That he didn't plan to settle down and have children? That he enjoyed picking up and exploring the world – all while hopefully bringing about some change and good through his documentaries? His movies were his children; he had dedicated his life to trying to make a difference for the habitats he explored, places that were threatened by the ever-creeping mass consumerism that seemed determined to exploit every last inch of this world. But more than one woman had thought she would be the one to make him want to retire to suburbia and raise kids behind the white picket fence.

Roman hated fences.

Avery would understand, Roman thought, rolling to his side and punching the pillow sack stuffed with his sweatshirt. She actually cared about the environment and worked to make it better. He doubted she would settle for some accountant somewhere who'd want to just shove her in the corner and dim her light. Hell, he doubted she even wanted a relationship. Based on his observations, she didn't seem the least bit interested in even being on this show. Why had she come here? What made her put herself in this situation that seemed so far out of her comfort zone? She always looked like a deer caught in headlights, constantly blindsided by the ridiculousness of some of these women's antics. Most of the rest of the cast were seasoned pros, sharpening their claws on each other and out for the big prize at the end. But Avery? She bumbled along all big-eyed, like a fawn taking its first steps.

Yet she'd been fantastic today, at least according to

his cameramen. What a shitshow, Roman thought, rubbing his hand over his face again, the fatigue settling in on his shoulders. When it rains, it pours, and today had been a monsoon. It was like everything had happened simultaneously and he'd been left scrambling to figure out the best care for everyone. The allergic reaction had taken top priority, because it wouldn't do to have one of the cast die under his watch. While his cameramen had restrained the two women fighting, he'd been administering an EpiPen and calling for an ambulance. At least the fighting women had given up and dissolved into puddles of tears within moments, negating the threat of them assaulting each other further. But, in his estimation, there was a lawsuit waiting to happen between them. The one with the broken nose wasn't likely to let that slide, especially if it marred her looks. Roman could just see the attorney now, arguing that her future earnings rested on the precision of her beautiful nose and the money her face brought in.

Roman needed a break.

As sleep crept up to claim him, Roman couldn't help but think about Avery, her eyes wide and shining in the moonlight, her lips as kissable as any he'd ever seen, and how it had taken everything in his power not to devour her lips on the spot. He wanted – no, *ached* for her, and having her plastered against his chest, gasping as if he'd just spent hours pleasuring her, had almost brought him to his knees.

If he hadn't known better, he might have thought Avery was the siren, and that the song she sang had lured him to her. Her magic was no less strong than the ethereal music that had danced across the moonlit waves.

He wondered if she had any idea of the power she wielded.

CHAPTER 23

"*U*gh, my head hurts," Cherylynn complained, pushing her tangled hair from her face.

"Box wine will do that to a person." Lisette nodded sagely, though Avery noticed she had her sunglasses on, even though the sun was just now cresting over the cliffs behind them, casting its gentle morning rays across the beach. The water was calm, lapping softly at the sand, and the events of last night seemed almost like a dream to Avery.

"Anyone else want some Advil?" she offered, having already unwrapped and checked Sara's foot and given her more pills for the swelling and pain.

"I love you. I shall name my firstborn after you," Cherylynn promised, falling dramatically back to the sand and putting the back of her hand to her forehead.

"Dramatic much?" Avery giggled, standing over her and handing her a couple of pills.

"Always, darling, always. Life is too boring not to

add a little drama now and then," Cherylynn said, gulping the pills down with what water was left in her bottle.

"We're also probably dehydrated. We didn't have much water to go around," Avery said, unwrapping a granola bar and taking a bite of her breakfast. They'd rationed some for this morning, and now all the women chewed in companionable silence. Avery mulled over whether she should tell them that she had seen Roman the night before. She saw no reason not to, but decided to leave some of their more interesting interactions out. She cleared her throat. "So, um, I spoke with Roman last night."

"Did you? How?" Sara asked, from her hammock.

"Was that where you went in the middle of the night? I swear I panicked when I woke up and saw you missing," Cherylynn said, still lying flat on her back in the sand and staring up at the sky.

"I went to pee, I told you that."

"And Roman watched you pee?"

"Ew, no. He came up to me when I was walking back. He just wanted to tell me that he was here, and to fill me in on what happened."

"He's here? Where?" Lisette craned her neck to look around and Avery did the same.

"I imagine he's up and gone by now. He said they'd bring help this morning."

"Thank god." Sara breathed a huge sigh of relief.

"What took them so long?" Cherylynn complained.

"Good question. I have a little gossip for you

ladies." Avery grinned as they all leaned in. "Remember that fight we saw yesterday?"

"Oh – what happened?" Lisette asked, unbraiding her hair and running her hand through some of the knotted strands that had come loose.

"Apparently one of the girls broke the other one's nose."

"No!" Lisette gasped, holding her hand to her own nose in shock. "That's... that's just over the line. That's the moneymaker right there."

"The moneymaker?" Avery asked, tilting her head at Lisette in question.

"Yeah, the moneymaker. You don't think most of these women are making money from regular day jobs, do you? Especially the influencers. Their currency is their looks. A broken nose can take down someone's career."

"That's..." Avery was going to say that it was a little sad and depressing, but then she remembered that Lisette classified herself as an influencer, so she decided to respond with empathy. "That's really awful then. Of course, I don't really think assault is cool, no matter what. I never was one who thrilled after violence. I don't like seeing people fighting."

"Me either, honey. I swear, Texans are a blood-thirsty bunch. They always want to settle things the tough way. Me? I'd rather pick flowers and give someone a hug than break a beer bottle and hold it to their throats."

"So what happens now? Are they disqualified from

the show? I'm sure there's something in the terms about violence," Lisette asked.

"I didn't ask. He also said that another woman got hit by a stingray and had an allergic reaction."

"Shut up! That's so scary. Yeah, you gotta do the stingray shuffle if you walk into the ocean." Lisette nodded.

"What in the hell is the stingray shuffle?" Cherylynn demanded. "It sounds like the macarena or a line dance."

"Shuffle to the left... no sting, no sting!" Avery chanted and the girls laughed.

"It's just an ocean thing. You shuffle your feet in the sand when you walk out. Any stingrays around will swim on, and you won't step directly on them. They're more scared of you than you of them."

"Didn't Steve Irwin die of a stingray sting?" Sara asked.

"Yes, to the heart. But he was also interacting too closely with them. The thing is, it's best to just observe the wildlife, especially in the ocean. Wave to them from afar. No touching," Lisette said.

"I have zero interest in touching a stingray," Sara promised.

"Some people do. They try to be cool and grab the rays, or a starfish. Did you know if you pull a starfish out of the water it suffocates in like seconds? All those people holding up starfish for their Instagram selfies are killing it. For what? A photo? It's stupid," Lisette said.

Avery found herself liking the woman even more. "I

didn't know that. I thought they could go out of the water," Avery said.

"Nope, they can't. They stress easily and suffocate. They basically have to hold their breath when they're being held out of the water. How long can you hold your breath for? Not long, that's for sure. It's one of my pet peeves with people around the ocean." Lisette shook her head.

"Gosh, I honestly never thought of it like that. I thought they were just like a shell or something," Cherylynn said.

"Nope. They are very much alive, and people kill them all the time being stupid," Lisette said.

"Look, there's Roman," Avery said, her attention caught by movement down the beach.

Roman walked across the sand in loose cargo shorts, a faded grey t-shirt, and sunglasses covering his eyes again. Behind him came two men with a stretcher.

"Where did they come from?" Lisette asked.

"I think from around the side of the cliff. See where you can walk on the sand now that the water is low again?" Sara said. She looked relieved to see the stretcher. Avery imagined her ankle was more painful than she was letting on.

"Good morning, ladies. I trust you slept well?" Roman asked when he stopped in front of them. Something about his nearness made Avery nervous, and her mind flitted back to the dream she'd had after she'd left his side last night.

Skin on skin... lips trailing down each other's

bodies. Heat throbbed, intense, between her legs, and she'd risen up over him, taking him inside her and claiming him as her own. Her face flamed as it all came back to her in vivid glory, and she turned away to busy herself with taking her hammock down and getting her pack ready. It wouldn't do for Roman to think he had that kind of effect on her, she reminded herself. She was in this game to win Beckett's heart and the cash prize.

I can't stop watching you, he'd said.

Was he watching her now? Did she look a mess? Avery ran a hand over her tangle of curls, then mentally berated herself. Of course she was a mess. They'd clambered over rocks in the dark, she'd dashed into the ocean in the middle of the night, and she'd slept on the beach in the night breezes. There was no way she was looking her best right now.

"The wine helped." Cherylynn, still lying on the ground, smiled up at Roman. "Is that stretcher for me? I could use some strong men to carry me out of here." The men holding the stretcher grinned down at Cherylynn, and she grinned right back at them.

"Sadly, no. You'll need to deal with your self-inflicted pain yourself," Roman said with a smile. He walked to Sara and crouched by her hammock. "How's the foot today?"

"It's really sore. I could use some more ice."

"We'll get you out of here. We have a Jeep right around the cliff to take you to the doctor and drop everyone back at the villa."

"Woo-hoo! You are my savior." Cherylynn bounced

up and did a little happy dance on the sand, then brought her hand to her head. "Okay, I moved too fast there. Owwww."

"Glad I can be your hero. You ready to go?" Roman asked Sara.

"Yes, I am." Sara let Roman lift her from the hammock and place her on the board between the two men, and they set off across the sand. Avery pretended she hadn't noticed how Roman's muscles had flexed in his arms when he'd lifted Sara, like she weighed no more than bag of rice.

"Let me just get her hammock down and I think that's our stuff all packed," Avery said. She moved to unknot the rope from the tree, but Roman was already there, his hands brushing hers. "Oh, sorry."

"It's fine, I'm happy to help." Roman cast a small smile at her and Avery turned. She stumbled, tripping over a root in the ground, and Roman caught her at the waist, steadying her. "Careful, we don't need another twisted ankle."

"Right, right. Sorry. I'm sure you've had your fill of injuries," Avery said, heat lacing her cheeks. She wanted to duck her head in the sand like an ostrich, but instead she took a deep breath and moved carefully to the other tree to untie the other side of the hammock.

Smooth, Avery, real smooth, she thought. Then she caught Cherylynn looking between the two of them, a small smile on her face. "How's that head of yours, Cherylynn?"

"It feels like someone took a hammer to my temple.

I'll be right as rain after a bloody Mary and two coffees. Oh, and maybe a shower. We got time for that today, Roman?"

"After the events of last night? Yeah, we have time for that today. We'll film an elimination ceremony tonight, but once we're back at the villa, I think everyone needs a few hours to recoup."

"Have I told you you're my hero?" Cherylynn purred.

"A few times. But don't stop."

"I wouldn't dream of it. Has anyone ever told you that you're quite the catch?" Cherylynn continued, twirling her hair around a finger.

Avery felt annoyance spike her gut. Why was she flirting with Roman? Wasn't she supposed to be making a play for Beckett?

"I can name quite a few women who would beg to differ." Roman grinned, looking like he was enjoying the flirtation – much to Avery's annoyance.

"How many women? Tell me, Roman, do you have a torrid past? You seem like you might, being a world-weary traveler and all. Maybe you just haven't met the right woman yet," Cherylynn cooed at him.

Avery found her hand itching to smack her. Surprised at the impulse, she bent to her pack, carefully folding the hammock into the smallest ball possible. What was wrong with her? She was not someone who would ever default to violence.

"Maybe I haven't," Roman agreed. "Most women

try to change me. They think I'll give up traveling and settle down to make babies and work an office job."

"You can't cage the stallion," Cherylynn nodded. "They work better when they're allowed to roam free."

"I'm not quite sure I get that analogy, but yes, I'm not built for that type of lifestyle. Maybe someday I'll find a woman who understands that."

"I like to travel," Cherylynn said.

"Cherylynn, would you stop getting this man all flustered and get to walking? I want a shower and some coffee," Lisette cut in.

Avery could have hugged her.

"Fine, fine. Let's go," Cherylynn laughed.

"I wasn't flustered," Roman said. "I don't mind when pretty women flirt with me."

"Duly noted." Looking over her shoulder, Cherylynn sent him as sultry a look as she could manage for being hungover and covered in sand and grit.

CHAPTER 24

"Just what was it you think you were doing back there?" Avery demanded once she and Cherylynn were back in their room. Both women had showered and had a cup of coffee, and Avery'd had time to stew on Cherylynn's flirting with Roman.

"You're going to need to clarify, hon. I'm too tired to play guessing games," Cherylynn said, her voice seeming extra sweet to Avery. Avery narrowed her eyes at her friend, who lounged on the bed, her feet kicked up and an arm thrown over her face.

"You know what I mean."

"I most certainly do not."

"Yes, you do. The flirting," Avery said, now annoyed with herself for being annoyed. Why couldn't she just let it go? What did it even matter?

"What? With the paramedics? They were cute. So what?"

"Not the paramedics." Avery breathed through her nose, wanting to scream.

"You'll need to be more specific, then. I flirt with everyone."

"You know what I am talking about."

"Avery, just spit it out." Cherylynn sighed and took the arm away from her face, rolling to look at Avery. "I can't possibly guess at what's bothering you if you don't use your words."

"With Roman!" Avery exploded.

Cherylynn sat up, jabbing her finger in the air at Avery. "Aha! I knew it! I knew you liked him!"

Avery's mouth dropped open. "I most definitely do not like him," she said, glaring at Cherylynn.

"Then why are you bothered that I flirted with him?"

"Because we're supposed to be flirting with Beckett," Avery said, smoothing the sheet on her bed and ignoring Cherylynn's knowing look.

"I flirt with him too," Cherylynn offered.

"I doubt that flirting with the producer of the show is going to put you in the running to win," Avery said.

"And I think you like Roman and you're not admitting it to me."

"I do not like Roman. The man is infuriating," Avery scoffed, looking away from Cherylynn. Getting up, she crossed the room and looked out over the water.

"Yeah, well, that's how you know you like someone," Cherylynn said.

"No. That's how you know you *don't* like someone," Avery clarified, turning and crossing her arms to look at

Cherylynn. "Listen, he annoys me, okay? He asks all these questions and is pushy with me. I don't like it. That's all. And I don't think you should flirt with him when you're supposed to be wooing another man."

"And I think you're lying to yourself. I flirted with him on purpose because I wanted to see your reaction. And now you're trying to sell both of us on some B.S."

"I'm not lying to myself. I just don't like him. And he's not a good match for you."

"I know that. But he could be a good one-night stand."

"Ugh! You're impossible. You can't just hook up with a producer on a dating show!" Avery fumed.

"Can't I?"

"But... seriously, are you saying you like him?"

Cherylynn sighed and pinched her nose.

"No, Avery. I'm saying *you* like him and you're clearly lying to yourself and to me. Which is fine – I'm not going to force you to admit feelings that you aren't ready to acknowledge. But when you're ready to talk about it, I'm here for you, okay?"

"I don't need... I don't... it's not..."

Avery felt her emotions well up inside and she didn't know what to think. A knock at their door prevented her from speaking further.

"Interview time, Avery." An intern nodded to Cherylynn and added, "You're up after her."

"Now? I was told we'd have the day to relax," Avery exclaimed, looking down at the swimsuit and loose coverup she'd pulled on after her shower. Her hair rained down in wet ringlets around her head and she hadn't put a drop of makeup on. Not to mention the fact that she couldn't bring herself to face Roman right now – not after what Cherylynn had just said.

"You do, after your interviews. It won't take long." The intern looked at his watch. "But you need to come down now. Cherylynn, come down in twenty minutes, please."

"Yes, sir." Cherylynn nodded and then turned to look at Avery after he'd left the doorway. "Good luck."

"I can't believe you put this in my head."

"Hon, it was already in your head or you wouldn't be madder than a cat that fell in a bathtub right now."

Throwing her hands up, Avery left the room, not even bothering to look in the mirror first. It wasn't like this show was going to portray her at her best, anyway. She stomped down the deathtrap staircase and entered the side room where they'd set up the interview space for both interviews and confessionals. She'd seen more than one woman go in there and blab away to the camera, presumably doing a confession, though the very idea made Avery cringe.

"You didn't mention we'd be doing interviews today," Avery said, plopping into the seat across from Roman and glaring at him. He looked great, much to her annoyance, fresh from the shower with a clean shirt pulled tight over his muscles.

"It's part of the gig, Avery. We've discussed this. These little interviews will serve as narration through the show. I know they aren't your favorite, but it's part of the deal," Roman said, patient as ever, as the cameramen adjusted their lights and got ready.

"Fine, let's make it quick then," Avery said, glancing down at her outfit. "I wasn't prepared to be on camera."

"You're always on camera here. Best not to forget that. Plus, you look great. Don't fuss too much."

With her list of complaints exhausted, Avery waited miserably for the questions he would fire at her. When the cameraman signaled the go-ahead, he began.

"Avery, can you tell us how you knew how to handle Sara's ankle injury? What was going through your head when she fell?"

"I was worried she was hurt very seriously," Avery said, crossing her legs and looking at Roman. "And I was glad to see that she wasn't bleeding and didn't have any more serious injuries."

"And how did you know how to help her?"

"It's just a sprained ankle. I took an emergency first responder course, so I knew what to do." Avery shrugged.

"Why did you take a course like that? Was it required for your work?" Roman asked.

"Because I think it's good to be prepared." Avery shrugged a shoulder. There was no way in hell she'd talk about her accident on television. That fear was hers, and hers alone, to relive. It wasn't something to be brought out and examined in front of millions of people. "What I don't like is when people say they'll help and then they don't."

"Please elaborate," Roman said, his eyes steady on hers.

"Beckett was there. It was nice of him to help carry Sara to the top of the cliff, but then we never saw him again. He claimed he was going for help, but he never came back." Avery had almost decided to throw production under the bus as well, for not assisting a cast member, but decided against it. She already suspected she was not going to come across all that great during these interviews anyway.

"Did you need him to come back? Were you hoping for a knight in shining armor?"

"I can be my own knight in shining armor, thank you very much." Avery tossed her head, lifting her chin up and staring Roman dead in the eyes. "But what I don't like is when someone says they'll do something and then doesn't follow through."

"Has that happened to you in the past?"

"Hasn't it happened to everyone?" Avery rolled her eyes.

"With a boyfriend?" Roman prodded.

"Yes, Roman, I've had men let me down in my life before. Much like every woman out there ever. It's a part of life. It's a part of learning. You learn to trust your instincts about people, and who you can rely upon and who you can't."

"Do you think all men are unreliable?"

"No, of course not. I just said you learn to trust your instincts," Avery scoffed. "And frankly, just because a man was unreliable with you doesn't mean he won't learn to be different, or can't be reliable with the next person. Don't make me out to be some bitter and jaded man-hater. I'm not."

"I wasn't trying to do that."

"That seems like where the line of questioning was going. And I won't be led down that route. I've met just as many great men in my life as I've met bad ones. And if you edit this to make it look like I have a chip on my shoulder about men, I'll sue you."

"Um, I don't think you can do that." Roman smiled at her. "But it is noted."

"Why can't I sue you? If you hurt my reputation?" Avery demanded.

"Avery…" Roman pinched his nose and motioned for the cameramen to cut filming. "I'm not going to edit you to look like a manhater. And you can't sue, it's part of the terms of your contract. You agreed to be edited however we see fit. That's the nature of the game."

"Well, it's stupid," Avery said, pushing her lip out.

"Fine, it may be stupid. But again, why are you here? You're the only woman in this group who gives me this much trouble."

"How am I giving you trouble? I'm just speaking my mind, and I won't be backed into a corner."

"It's not backing you into a corner to ask you about your life. How am I – I mean how are the viewers supposed to get to know you?" Roman said, his face flashing with an emotion that Avery couldn't quite read.

"I'm sorry, I'm being a bitch." Avery sighed and ran

her hands over her face. "I'm tired and I'm being cranky again."

"Did you eat?" Roman asked.

"No. I was going to, but I got called in to interview."

"Okay. Making a note that I should only interview you after you've been well-fed."

Despite herself, Avery grinned.

"Don't you know that about women yet? We get cranky when we're hungry."

"Yes, so it seems. We'll pick up this interview later. Go feed yourself."

"I plan to. Sorry for my abrasiveness," Avery said. She stood at the same time Roman did. They paused, a mere six inches between them, and Avery caught her breath as she looked up into Roman's eyes. She wanted to ask him, again, if he had seen the mermaid last night or if she was slowly going crazy. But it was out of the question – not when the cameras were watching. The experience had been so breathtakingly beautiful that Avery wanted to hold it close to her heart, not take it out and pick it apart for its veracity.

"No problem. I'll remember this for the future," Roman said, clearing his throat and stepping back to let her pass. She brushed past him, feeling the warmth of his nearness, and paused at the door where Cherylynn stood.

"Feeling any better?" Cherylynn asked.

"Nope. I'm going to make a burrito and read my book," Avery said.

"That sounds like the perfect cure." Cherylynn patted her on the shoulder. "Oh, hi there, handsome…"

"I swear to god, Cherylynn," Avery hissed, and stormed away when Cherylynn threw back her head and laughed.

To hell with them both, Avery thought and zeroed in on the food table.

CHAPTER 25

*A*very did her best to avoid the other women, which didn't seem to take much as they all seemed to be giving her a wide berth for some reason. At this point, Avery didn't much care. She wasn't used to being around this many people for this long a time, and the effort of making conversation and managing people's emotions, including her own, was exhausting her.

After making a quick sandwich and filling her reusable water bottle, Avery shoved everything in her beach bag and hightailed it down the beach, far away from the cameras and where she thought they were allowed to go. She didn't really care, since they were busy doing interviews anyway and they'd been told they could have a day off.

It wasn't a shock to Avery that she needed a break from everyone. Ruby had always been the extrovert of the two, while Avery consistently needed time alone to recharge her batteries. Even on family trips, Avery would disappear after a few days together and hole up with a book for a few hours, needing the space to not speak to anyone. Today was one of those days, and Avery knew if she didn't take this break now she'd be nothing but horrible the rest of the time.

Finding a shaded spot under a palm tree, she threw her towel down, leaned back against the tree, and just closed her eyes, letting her brain wander. She was too keyed up to focus on reading her book, so instead she just practiced some deep breathing exercises to bring some calm to the storm that seemed to rage inside her. Opening her eyes, she dug into her bag and ate her food, not really tasting it, and stared out at the crystal blue water.

What was she doing on this island? On this show even? She was an adult woman, capable of saying no to her sister. There was no reason she should have felt forced into taking this spot on a reality show. Avery didn't even like reality shows. And yet here she was, once again rushing to her sister's aid. What was it in her that felt the need to take care of Ruby?

Perhaps if she was so focused on fixing Ruby, she wouldn't have to focus on fixing herself. At that uncomfortable thought, Avery put the bag of chips down and wrapped her arms around her knees, pulling them to her chest. Hugging herself, essentially.

So maybe her natural inclination toward introversion

had gone a little far after her accident, Avery acknowledged, as she looked out across the beautiful water once more. Aside from going to work and the gym, she rarely socialized unless Ruby dragged her out. It shocked her to realize that maybe Ruby had been more of a crutch for her than she'd realized. No wonder she'd taken off to travel around the world, Avery sniffed. Here she'd thought of Ruby as someone she had to take care of – even a burden, at times – and it was likely that her sister felt the same exact way about her. Perhaps that wasn't the most comfortable revelation, but there it was.

"You look like you're mulling over something."

Avery blinked up at Irma, not having even seen the woman approach. She shook her head as though to clear the clouds from her mind.

"I am, kind of. Just some uncomfortable truths is all."

"Mind if I join you?" Irma asked. She was stunning in a flowing blue dress with pretty red beading on the straps. Her long grey hair was bound with a leather cord, and numerous bracelets jingled merrily on her wrists.

"Please do," Avery said, shifting so Irma could lean against the tree as well if she chose. Instead, Irma sat to her side, looking half at Avery and half out at the sea.

"It's a nice spot for reflection. I come here often to do so."

"I can't imagine you have much to reflect on. You seem entirely too put-together and wise to have any problems." Avery winced at the way that sounded and held her hand up. "I'm sorry. That sounded rude. I have no idea where my filter's gone today."

"Everyone has problems. Even us wise old folks." Irma smiled.

"You're not old, you're timeless," Avery said, smiling back at her.

"Be that as it may, I am still older than you. And I know a sulking woman when I see one. I have two daughters who are experts at it."

"Is that what I'm doing? Sulking? Maybe." Avery shrugged. "I guess I just needed some space from all the chatter and gossip to clear my head. I'm used to spending more time alone, and I like quiet spaces. It's why I like being in nature so much. Fewer distractions."

"I can understand that. It must be tough sharing that villa with so many strong personalities."

"It is. But I think what I'm realizing is that it's also good for me. I've had some hard truths I think I needed to confront. I'm not totally there yet, but I'm starting to."

"Want to tell me about it?" Irma asked, and Avery found that she did.

She told her everything. Starting with her accident, she led Irma all the way up to the point last night where she had seen the mermaid. There she stopped, not sure if she should continue.

"Did something catch your attention?" Irma urged her on.

"I... I think you may think I'm silly," Avery said.

"Silly is not the word that comes to mind for you.

Brave. Strong. Those are words that come to mind when I think of your journey."

"Ha – thanks, but not really. I'm not even being truthful with Roman about who I am," Avery said, picking at a blade of grass at the base of the tree. "I'm here on false pretenses."

"Well, a bit, yes, but you haven't misrepresented who you are as a person. Sure, you're not Ruby, but you aren't pretending to be Ruby's personality or job or anything else. I'd say it's a fairly small thing, when it all comes down to it. Unless you're hiding more?" Irma peered at her.

"No, I'm not. Everything else has been true, except my name. And I've told people I came here on a dare, which is pretty close to the truth anyway, since all this is quite daring for me." Avery sighed, and trailed the blade of grass over her toes one by one. "I think Ruby was right, though. I may have needed this."

"Sometimes we need a nudge or two to get us unstuck. There's nothing wrong with that."

"Going on a reality TV show in another country is more than a nudge."

"Fine – some of us need a swift kick in the ass to get back to living life. And it sounds like you did. Now, what were you saying about last night? You stopped so suddenly when you were talking about being awoken from a deep sleep. Was everything all right?"

"I… oh god, you're going to think I'm crazy." Avery buried her face in her hands for a moment and then rested her chin on her knees, meeting Irma's calming eyes.

"Try me."

"Um, well, I think I might have seen the... siren of Siren Island? Not the rocks that everyone talks about. But like... um, well, a real, actual mermaid?" Avery's voice squeaked at the end of that, and she couldn't actually believe she was saying that out loud.

"It's entirely possible," Irma nodded, shocking Avery to her core.

"You can't be saying... wait... no way," Avery said, joy blooming deep in her core. It seemed silly, sure, but believing in mermaids was not a gift she'd ever thought she would get in this lifetime. It was kind of like a child believing in Santa Claus and all his little elves. The joy around that idea was just so untouched and pure. Eventually, it wore off, as people were told that Santa wasn't real. But... this... this was something that maybe nobody could take from her. If she just allowed herself to *actually* believe it.

"I am saying it. What did it feel like to you?" Irma asked, her eyes still holding Avery's.

"It felt real," Avery admitted. "And I woke up wishing it hadn't all been a dream."

"Why do you think it was a dream? You just told me it felt real."

"Because... but..." Avery stammered, "It's hard for me to believe that mermaids are real. I want to believe they are. I feel like they could be."

"So why don't you let yourself believe?"

"Irma, you're driving me crazy here. Please, can you just tell me if you believe they're real?" Avery begged. She was too tired and too on-edge to go in circles.

"Of course I believe they're real."

"You do?"

"Unequivocally, yes."

"You've seen them, then?" Avery asked.

"Of course," Irma said, a knowing smile crossing her beautiful face. Though lines creased her skin and luscious grey hair, Avery couldn't have imagined a more beautiful woman sitting in front of her. If anything, her age and wisdom made her more stunning. She almost seemed to glow, much like the mermaid last night, while Avery stared at her in shock.

"I swear, you could be a mermaid." Avery laughed, shaking her head at her ridiculousness. "You just glow."

"Who says I'm not?" Irma said.

Avery's eyes widened. "Um, what would you be doing on land if you were?"

"Who says mermaids can't be on land?"

"I don't know… I thought all the myths and legends said mermaids had to stay in the water."

"Sometimes. Not all the time," Irma said, shrugging a delicate shoulder.

"Irma, you're kind of rocking my world a bit right now. I… I just… okay. You're a pretty badass woman, from what I can tell. You're smart. You're stunning. You're kind. And you're telling me that without a doubt you believe mermaids to be real. As in actual living beings, not mythological characters, that exist in the here and now."

"Yes."

"And you've seen them."

"Of course. Many of us here have. Ask the local fishermen. They'll swear up and down they've seen them."

"You're saying, without a doubt, that what I saw last night was real?" Hope blossomed in Avery's chest. She wanted to hold onto that moment, the beauty and heartache and otherworldliness of it all as her secret for the rest of her life. It had been a gift, like no other, and maybe, just maybe, it would be enough for her to believe in magic again.

"Of course. It's lovely they showed themselves to you. It means you're pure of heart."

"Reallllly?" Avery almost squealed.

"Really." Irma laughed and squeezed her arm. "Don't doubt yourself so, Avery. You've had a rough journey, and you're just learning how to blossom again. The mermaids choose who they show themselves to very carefully. It's a gift."

"It felt that way. But… her song. Her song was almost heartbreaking. A song of longing. I wanted to go to her and comfort her," Avery said, her eyes huge. She stared out at the sea, knowing she would forever look at the ocean in a completely different way.

"Which is why she shared that song with you. Not everyone would think to comfort a mermaid. They'd try and take a photo of her, video her, or even capture her.

But you wanted to help her. What do you think that says about you?"

"I… I don't know. I was just caught up in the moment. Why is she so sad?"

"I think they like you. And, maybe, you needed to hear her song. There's beauty in sadness, as well, you know. If we don't long for something, ache for something, how do we know it's real? Love isn't pure joy. Love isn't just a comfort blanket. Love can also bring sadness and melancholy. It's a huge emotion, after all – and, as we all must come to terms with, everything changes. Nothing we love stays. And that's a sadness that many people can't grasp. What humans don't always understand, though, is that the emotion – love, in itself? That never goes away. It's a part of the fabric of the universe. Once you love, it gets woven into all of time. You see, the memory of your love is imprinted on the world, forever changing the course of history. She wasn't singing because her heart was broken, you see? She was singing because her heart was full."

"Oh," Avery said. Her eyes filled with tears, emotion pulsing through her in waves. "She really did give me a gift."

"She did. And I hope you'll treasure it always."

"I swear I will, Irma. I want to do right by her."

"You don't have to do right by her. You have to do right by yourself. Live your own truth, Avery. No more hiding under a rock. No more comfort zones. Turn your petals to the sun, and blossom."

Long after Irma had left her, with promises to see

her soon, Avery sat there, eyes on the horizon, searching for her mermaid. And even though she didn't come, Avery knew she'd always carry a piece of her inside. With a newfound sense of purpose – heck, even lightness to her step – Avery finally left her spot and danced the whole way back to the villa.

CHAPTER 26

"Well, you're looking a bit perkier," Cherylynn said when Avery bounced back into the room. She let out a little gasp of surprise when Avery bounded across the room and threw her arms around her friend's shoulders.

"I'm sorry I was such a crotchety bitch," Avery said, giving Cherylynn a big smooch on the cheek. "I'll work on being better."

"Now what in the hell has gotten into you? Have you been drinking?" Cherylynn said, raising an eyebrow at Avery and giving her a little attitude. Avery didn't blame her; she'd been quite rude earlier.

"I have not. Though maybe we should go have a glass of wine by the pool."

"Now you're talking my language. Rosé all day."

"Erm, maybe not all day. But, yes, I'm sorry I was so cranky with you."

"It's fine – I was kind of poking the bear anyway."

Cherylynn sighed and stood up. "We gotta get ready for our night ceremony anyway. Elimination time. Now, what's put you in such a good mood?"

"Is it that late already? Jeez, where did the time go?" Avery said, moving to her bedside table and pulling out the book her sister had given her. Paging through it, she found the outfit she was supposed to wear and went to dig it from the closet.

"I don't know, but from the looks of it, you must've had a good shag or something to put you in a good mood."

"I wish I had a good shag. It's been years," Avery admitted, then whipped around at Cherylynn's shocked gasp. "What's wrong?"

"I'm sorry… I think my heart may have stopped for a second. Did you say it's been years since you've been with a man?"

"Correct," Avery said.

"Bless your heart, no wonder you're cranky," Cherylynn decided, sending Avery into fits of laughter.

"I'm sure that's a contributing factor."

"It would be for me. Honey, why are you restricting yourself from eating at the buffet? There's loads of men out there to sample."

"I'm starting to realize that I've been hiding under my rock for a little too long," Avery admitted, turning back to the closet and digging through until she pulled out a shimmery turquoise dress that swept all the way to the floor in one fluid column of silk.

"Well, this sure is one way to come out to play. But

I'm wondering if you're focusing on the wrong man," Cherylynn prodded.

"Okay, listen – yes, I think about Roman. Mostly he annoys me. But I'd be lying if I said I didn't find him attractive."

"Well, duh. I've got eyes in my head, don't I? I'd like to lick him like an ice cream cone. That man is dee-licious," Cherylynn said.

"But Beckett is handsome too," Avery quickly amended.

"Sure he is. They all are. There's even a cute cameraman I have my eye on. Until I have a ring on this finger" – Cherylynn held up her left hand – "smor-gasbord."

"I will take that under consideration."

"So what are you going to do about Roman?"

"I'm doing nothing about Roman. There's nothing to be done. I'm going to stay in this reality show, see if I can actually get to know Beckett and find out if there's more to him than just some California surfer bro, and I'm going to give it an honest shot. That's all I can really do, right?"

"Yeah... but what if you miss out on love right in front of your face?"

"How can it be love, Cherylynn? We snipe at each other more often than not."

"From where I'm sitting, you're the one doing the sniping. He's just trying to get to know you better. You sort of have this 'approach with caution' vibe going on."

"I do?"

"Yeah, like – don't get me wrong, you're gorgeous. But you're kind of like a rose… really, really pretty, but if you get too close the thorns'll cut you."

"That might be the nicest thing anyone's ever said to me," Avery decided.

"I'm not really sure it was a compliment?" Cherylynn huffed out a laugh.

"No, really, I don't mind being tough. I think I've needed to be. But it's nice to know that I'm not all tough, you know? And I can work on it. I'll get better. I'll try to be more open. I need to not hide so much anymore."

"Well, whatever happened to you today – I like it," Cherylynn decided, motioning for Avery to sit on the bed so she could do her hair. "And I hope that, no matter what, we'll remain friends once this is over."

"Of course we will. I want to come see this ranch of yours."

"You're always welcome. We'll get you in a saddle soon enough. But seriously, friends, right?"

"Friends, promise."

"Even if one of us wins? No resentment?"

"No resentment. I promise. It's such a long shot of me winning anyway that I don't think I'll be fussed if I lose. I'd rather have someone I like win the prize."

"Me too. I don't think I could stand it if that fake girl from Brooklyn won."

A gong sounded from below – their fifteen-minute warning – and Cherylynn screeched.

"Shoot, you're going to have to finish up yourself."

Avery changed quickly into her dress, leaving her hair as Cherylynn had done it – a simple braid circling her crown and the rest tumbling over her shoulders. Looking in the mirror, she smudged some shadow on her eyes, making them look a little larger, and swiped a coat of mascara on. Digging in her jewelry pouch, she found a long turquoise pendant to wear and some dripping golden waterfall-style earrings. On a whim, she placed a cuff of gold on her upper arm, feeling a bit like a goddess in her dress, and stepped back to survey the results.

"You look great," Cherylynn said, rushing out of the bathroom.

"Thanks, so do you. I love that color pink on you," Avery said, admiring the one-shoulder gown that skimmed Cherylynn's body.

"Thanks. Okay, we have to move it, sister," Cherylynn said, grabbing Avery by the hand and tugging her downstairs. They followed the group of girls out to the pool deck, where flame torches were lit, with a perfect view of the sun kissing the horizon. Beckett stood by Jack, looking handsome this evening in a loose linen suit coat thrown casually over his t-shirt.

"He looks nice," Avery said to Cherylynn, and she nodded her agreement.

"Good evening, ladies," Jack said, commencing the evening ceremony.

Avery felt the wave of tension roll over the group. She'd avoided people most of the day, but some of the gossip about the other groups' adventures had wafted back to her anyway. She suspected tonight was going to be one dramatic ceremony. "As you know, tonight is an elimination ceremony. We've had a particularly eventful couple of days, so let's review a bit of what happened on the screen here."

Avery looked over to the screen that had been rolled out on a stand next to the pool's edge. They all watched as the clip rolled of the fight that had broken out between the women.

"I can't believe that girl got her nose broken for pointing out someone's cellulite," Avery whispered to Cherylynn, honestly shocked that a comment like that had led to bloodshed. And oh my, had blood been shed. A bright spurt of blood had flown from the poor girl's nose. Avery craned her head to see the woman, her nose bandaged and both her eyes blackened, staring sullenly at the screen.

"I can't either. But in all fairness, the other girl shoved her first."

"That's true, but jeez, was that really that necessary?" The other woman looked smug, clearly convinced that she would be staying around for another round.

"Ladies." Beckett stepped forward to address the two who had been in the fight. "I do not like or approve of violence in any fashion. Hurting each other, especially for something so silly, not only shows me your character, but also what it would be like to have an argument with you. As you know, in any relationship, there are arguments, and if you resort to violence to resolve them – well, I want no part of that. Neither of you will move to the next round, and I ask that you both leave immediately. Please begin packing your bags now."

The smug girl's mouth dropped open, and tears ran down the face of the one with the black eyes. They both turned and stomped off, a cameraman and a security guard following them, presumably to break up any fights that occurred next.

"Let that be a lesson to the rest of you. Violence is never the answer," Beckett said. "This challenge was about teamwork. A relationship is like being on a team and working together to achieve a goal is really important. With that in mind, I'd like to congratulate the winners, who not only found the treasure, but also overcame an injury to do so."

The women cheered, though Avery could tell that much of it was fake. She smiled anyway, high-fiving Cherylynn, Lisette, and Sara, who sat on the sofa with her leg in a brace and real crutches by her side. As they'd thought, it was just a nasty sprain, and Avery was happy to see the color back in Sara's cheeks. They must have given her some good pain meds.

"I've also made the decision to send the other two teams home," Beckett said. He watched the group carefully as a sudden silence drifted across the room.

"What… but… we're supposed to be here for a while," one woman said, confusion crossing her face.

"I know. But I think I can make my decision by narrowing it down to a small number of women and really spending time with each one on my own. This is about love, after all, and it's more important to me that I take my time figuring this out."

"Holy shit," Cherylynn whispered. "I've never seen something like this happen before. The producers have to be shitting themselves."

Avery glanced around for Roman, but couldn't find him.

"The people who stay can vote one person back on, right?" one woman pointed out.

"They can. And that would bring it down to five women, all of whom I can take my time getting to know." Beckett smiled.

"But… so you're saying you don't even want to give one of us a chance? You barely got to know us!" One woman slammed her champagne glass on the floor where it shattered into pieces, then she stomped away from the pool. The brunette next to her, Georgette, winced and bent down to her foot.

"I think that says all I need to know about you," Beckett called after her.

"I… I don't mean to interrupt," Georgette said, "but her glass cut my foot open."

"I'm sorry." Beckett rushed to her side. "How bad is it? Do you need stitches?"

"Maybe. It looks deep. But let's just finish this off. I'll put a napkin on it for now," Georgette said, remaining remarkably calm considering all the blood that flowed from her foot.

"She stays," Cherylynn said, looking around at their group. They all nodded. Cherylynn cleared her throat and raised her hand. "Beckett, we've decided who can stay."

"Go ahead," Beckett said. He was crouched by the woman's foot, pressing on it with his hand to stop the bleeding.

"I think Georgette should stay, considering she just took a piece of glass to the foot and smiled pleasantly through it all. I think that speaks of her character," Cherylynn said.

"Good choice," Beckett said.

Georgette beamed at their group while the rest of the women stormed off in a huff.

"I think… maybe we stay down here and have a glass of wine?" Lisette decided, eyeing the balcony above where furious voices were shouting.

"Oh yeah. You couldn't pay me a thousand dollars to go back up those stairs right now."

CHAPTER 27

The villa felt oddly empty with the smaller group that was left spread out across the rooms. Cherylynn and Avery had decided to continue sharing a room as they enjoyed each other's company, and neither could be bothered to pack all their stuff up just to move next door.

"I wonder where he'll take me," Cherylynn said, racing around the room with her hands full of bikinis. It looked like a bomb had gone off; clothes were scattered everywhere and about fifteen different sandals had been tossed across the floor. Avery briefly wondered how'd she managed to even pack fifteen pairs of shoes.

"I mean, it's an island. So there can only be so many places," Avery pointed out. "Maybe on a boat?"

"Oh… okay, so I'll need to plan for windy-day hair and if it gets cold on the water later."

"I mean, I don't actually know, Cherylynn. It was just a guess," Avery laughed. After Beckett's monumental decision to kick off most of the other women, the producers had met for a long meeting. Avery hadn't realized that Roman was working with another producer on the show, but she supposed it made sense to have more than one on set. Now Beckett had decided he wanted getaway dates with each woman, including an overnight, and that prospect made her entirely too nervous. Glad that she wasn't the first to be chosen, Avery was on standby to approve Cherylynn's outfit choices – not that she could offer a ton of assistance.

"What does that little book of yours say for overnight dates?" Cherylynn demanded, hands on hips, one strap of her tank top sliding down her shoulder.

"Um." Avery paged quickly through the book. "It has a couple options. But it's underlined and stressed and highlighted here that you should wear a lot of layers and remember you're on camera."

"Smart. If things heat up, clothes can come off slowly. If you're just wearing a maxi-dress, he can pull it right off and then you're naked to the world. Separates take time and keep you more covered." Cherylynn pursed her lips and studied the pile of clothes while Avery gaped at her.

"You're going to sleep with Beckett?"

"I don't know. Maybe. If I like him and the mood is right." Cherylynn shrugged, not catching Avery's expression. "I think that's kind of what these dates are about."

"But… you barely know him," Avery pointed out.

"So? Sex is sex. I'm allowed to take my own pleasure when I feel like it. I hate the antiquated notion that men can run around and sleep with all these women and they're just charmers or playboys, while women get labeled sluts if we do the same. I'm a modern woman, Avery. If I want to have sex with someone – someone I find attractive and think will give me pleasure, the way I demand it – then I have no qualms about taking what I want. There's absolutely nothing wrong with that. It just peeves me when people clutch their pearls and talk about 'loose women.' What about these loose men? Where's the pearl-clutching for them?"

"I… yes, I agree. It's certainly a misogynistic view of sex, isn't it? I'll admit I haven't given it much thought of late." Avery pursed her lips.

"Well, you've been on a bit of a dry spell. Self-imposed, mind you, self-imposed. I bet you couldn't walk ten paces out that front door without finding a man who'd be willing to pleasure you," Cherylynn said.

"Cherylynn! It's not… I mean… it should be a shared pleasure." Avery was kind of astounded to think about just using a man for her own pleasure. She'd cut herself off from exploring anything of that nature since her accident, and was now surprised to feel a trickle of interest pique her. Could she just… you know… let someone give her pleasure?

"If you think that a man isn't getting pleasure from giving, then you're picking the wrong man. They should enjoy making you happy, and you share pleasure together."

"She's absolutely right," Roman said, leaning

against the doorway, his arms crossed over his chest and a wicked grin on his face.

"Eeep!" Avery said and buried her face in the first thing she snatched from the bed. Unfortunately for her, it was a very red and very lacy bra.

"Especially if you wear something like that," Roman added. "A man should put the woman first. Well, a good one, at least."

"I knew I liked you, Roman," Cherylynn decided. She held up two different tops. "Green or gold?"

"Gold. Metallic makes you look shimmery and decadent. Plus it shows up well on camera."

"Thanks! I should have had you around more when I was planning out my outfits," Cherylynn said. Avery took advantage of their momentary distraction to shove the lacy bra under a pillow and smooth the hair from her face. She wondered how long he had been listening, and felt heat flush her cheeks again.

"Well, I'm happy to provide wardrobe assistance." Roman grinned again. "I'm here to tell you that Beckett is ready to leave. The crew is also ready."

"Is there anything else I need to know or should prepare for?"

"No, I don't think the date is anything too dramatic. I really think he wants to spend time getting to know you."

"Perfect – then I should be ready." Cherylynn surveyed the mess she'd left behind. "Sorry, Avery. This place is a mess."

"It's fine. I probably won't be in here long," Avery said. "Have fun!"

Cherylynn waved goodbye and bounced from the room.

Avery expected Roman to follow. Instead, he lounged at the door. "What are you doing with your day off?"

"Is it really a day off? As in, no cameras following me?" Avery asked, tilting her head in question at him.

"Well, if you stay here," Roman said, nodding up to the cameras tucked in the corners of the room, "you'll be on camera. Or anywhere on the villa. If you go offsite, you won't be. We don't have a large enough crew to follow everyone, and the real footage is following where Beckett goes."

"Could I like... I don't know, rent a scooter or something and tour the island? Is that allowed?"

"Of course it is. You aren't a prisoner here. Though I'd prefer you let me drive you around in the Jeep. I'm not a fan of scooters. Have you driven one before?"

"No, I haven't. They don't seem too tough." Avery dodged his offer of driving her around in a Jeep. Didn't he have to be on production?

"They're trickier than you think. People don't look for scooters when they're driving. I've seen a lot of nasty injuries from accidents with scooters."

"Nope, I don't want that. Maybe I can get a taxi or hire a car then," Avery said. She stood, tossing a few things in her bag. She already had her bathing suit and coverup on.

"Avery, I'd like to explore the island today. Would you like to join me?"

"Aren't you filming?"

"I'm off today," Roman said. "We have built-in days off during filming; otherwise we burn out."

"Oh," Avery said, pausing, not really sure what to do. Was this a date? Just friends? Should she be going on a date with another man when she was on a dating show? How would that look to Beckett?

"Just friends, Avery," Roman said, seeming to read her mind.

"Sure, okay, thank you. Yes, I'd love to get a chance to see more of the island," Avery admitted.

"Great – meet me downstairs in fifteen? I just have to make a call."

"Thank you, Roman. This is really nice of you."

"It's a gift to me as well. I'm getting a little stir-crazy in this house." Roman flashed her a smile and left.

Avery whirled, grabbing her little book of outfits and flipping through until she found one labeled "island day date." Not caring that she should probably save her look for a date with Beckett, she quickly packed her bag and changed her outfit.

Then she immediately changed back, because what would Roman think if she got herself all gussied up for him? It would look like she was trying too hard. Annoyed with herself, she grabbed her bag and left the room, excited for a friendly day out exploring.

Just friends, Avery repeated to herself, just friends.

CHAPTER 28

"Why are we stopping here?" Avery asked when Roman pulled the Jeep to a stop just a little bit down the road from their villa. Peering over his shoulder, she saw a sign that read "The Laughing Mermaid." "Oh, is this Irma's place? I've been wanting to see it."

True to their word, the women of the Laughing Mermaid had made themselves available as confidants and mentors to the group, but Avery only knew of a few who had actually taken them up on their offers of help. The general consensus seemed to have been that most of the women didn't want to be on camera next to such beauties. Avery didn't care much about that, and had always been delighted when she'd seen any of the women. Spending time with them felt like going home – she missed her sister so much she couldn't breathe at times, and having Irma, Jolie, and Mirra operate as a stand-in family had done wonders for her.

"It is," Roman replied. "Want to come in?"

"Of course." Avery was already halfway out of the vehicle. He'd taken the doors off the Jeep but had pulled the canvas top over so they still had shade.

"Come back to the kitchen," Irma's voice carried through the open front door.

Roman and Avery walked through a cool white-washed hallway decorated with stunning prints of the ocean, over to a large farm-style door that was rolled open. The kitchen – large, open-air, and done up in an almost Tuscan style – featured a massive wood table which dominated the room and invited people to settle in for a chat. Irma stirred something at the stove, resplendent as usual in a flowy peach dress with her hair done in braids. Jolie and Mirra – both looking like they'd stepped out of the pages of a magazine – sat at the table, carefully wrapping some cheese in butcher paper.

"I love this kitchen," Avery declared by way of greeting. "It feels so homey. I think that's what I don't like about the villa we're staying at."

"You don't like the villa?" Roman asked in surprise.

"Not really. It's very cold. White on white on white. We're in the Caribbean. Shouldn't there be splashes of color and fun?"

"I agree. I think it's important to infuse your decorating with some whimsy," Mirra said, placing the cheese in a cooler.

"Do you do all your own decorating?" Avery asked.

"We do. I think the personal touch helps. Granted, we live here too. The villa you're renting is owned by someone off-island as an investment property, so they probably designed it with what they thought was best for that. It's just our taste, is all," Jolie said, standing and crossing the room to pull a bottle of white wine from the fridge. She added it to the cooler.

"Where are you two off to today? Do you have a break from filming?" Irma smiled at Avery.

"I do! I mean, we do. I feel like a kid on holiday break," Avery confessed, laughing a little. "I'm not sure where we're going. Just to explore."

"There's a lovely little beach on the other side of the island with a really well-sheltered cove. I call it my swimming pool because the water is always so calm there. It might be nice for your picnic," Irma said.

"Our picnic?" Avery turned to Roman.

"I asked the ladies to put together a hamper for us. I've been lucky enough to have some of their home cooking before, and I thought it would be a treat," Roman said. He handed Irma some money, pressing a kiss to her cheek in thanks.

"Oh, let me contribute," Avery said. She glanced back down the hallway. "But my purse is in the car."

"It's on me," Roman said. "This is as much a treat for me as it is for you."

"It's all set then. Roman, why don't you take this to the car?" Irma nodded at the cooler and the picnic hamper.

"I know when I'm being dismissed," Roman laughed, and shouldered both items easily and disappeared outside.

"Do you like him?" Jolie asked immediately.

"Yeah, is this a date?" Mirra hissed, leaning to glance down the hallway to make sure Roman was out of sight.

"Girls," Irma cautioned, wiping her hands on a rag and then leaning back to cross her arms over her chest. "Well? Is it?"

"I don't think so. We agreed this was just as friends. We both wanted to get out and explore. I think other girls might join us too." Avery shrugged.

"But you like him," Jolie pressed.

"I… I don't dislike him," Avery said, dodging the question.

"She likes him." Jolie tossed a swath of her black hair over her shoulder. "Smart choice. He's great."

"I didn't say I liked him," Avery said, flushing. "It would be weird of me to go on a date with another man while I was on a dating show."

"Would it? I don't think any of these women are really in it to find love," Mirra said. "In fact, I don't think Beckett actually is either."

"Maybe not, but wouldn't it be disingenuous of me to not even try?" Avery wondered.

"Well, sure. I mean, go on your date with Beckett and see if you like him, but I think you already know how you feel about him – unless I'm reading you wrong?" Jolie narrowed her eyes at Avery and Avery felt a wave of… something pulse over her.

"What was that?" Avery asked, fluttering her hand a little in the air.

"Jolie's reading you to see if you're lying," Mirra said easily.

"Can you do that?" Avery demanded.

"Of course I can do that." Jolie shrugged.

"Girls, you're flustering Avery. That's enough," Irma said, and then came to stand in front of Avery. "Don't worry about what they say; they're just in love with love. They want everyone to be happy."

"Tell that to the women on the show who are jealous of them," Avery laughed.

"Simple women. They need to learn when to make allies and when to not be judgmental," Jolie sniffed.

"Enjoy your day, Avery." Irma raised her hand and made a motion to the door. "Don't put too much pressure on this. Or yourself. Be young. Have fun. See how you feel once the day is over. Just remember that nothing matters but love."

"Why do you keep saying love? I'm just… I don't know, I'm just here. I'm exploring. I'm having fun with a friend today," Avery griped.

"That word scares her," Mirra said to Jolie.

"It does. But that's okay. She'll be ready when she's ready," Jolie replied, as if Avery wasn't even there.

"I'm going to go now," Avery decided.

"Have fun today. We want full details." Mirra smiled

her angelic smile at Avery, and she found it impossible not to grin back.

"Has anyone ever told you two that you're trouble?" Avery asked.

"Only the best kind." Jolie winked.

"I don't doubt it."

CHAPTER 29

"Oh, let's stop there." Avery pointed at a cheerful hut by the water. Its door was thrown open and the shutters on the windows were painted all different colors.

"Yes, ma'am," Roman said, pulling the Jeep into the gravel lot next to the hut. They'd cruised the island for a little while, the radio playing music when it caught the signal, but hadn't spoken much. Avery found that she didn't mind riding in silence with Roman; it was nice not to have to fill every second with chatter.

"Oh, it's like a little gallery," Avery said. "Cool. Maybe we'll find some art."

"Do you like to pick up art when you travel?"

"I haven't been traveling much in the past few years, but yeah, I used to. Who needs a t-shirt that'll just get tossed in the back of a closet? I much prefer picking up some local art to remember the area by," Avery said.

She didn't see the questioning look Roman gave her as she walked in the door of the gallery.

"Welcome! I'm Lola and this is my space. I hope you'll enjoy looking around," said a woman from the back of the room where she was hammering at a frame on a long wood table. She was every bit as gorgeous as Mirra and Jolie.

"Hi, Lola. Your space is beautiful, as are you," Avery said.

Lola shot her a smile. "That's sweet of you. Are you here on vacation?"

"Something like that. He's working – but I'm on a reality show. I can't say it has been the most relaxing," Avery admitted, studying a trio of black and white photographs of cactus and birds.

"Ah yes, the show's been the talk of the town," Lola said. "You're working on it, then?"

"I'm the producer," Roman agreed.

Lola studied him for a moment. "Doesn't seem like your type of gig," she said.

Avery shot her a look. The woman was a good read.

"Why do you say that?"

"I'm a photographer. We study people. And you, good sir, do not scream 'reality television producer' to me."

"I am and I'm not," Roman grinned. "I'm good at producing them, but my heart lies in nature documentaries. I'm planning for this to be my last round of reality television – I'd promised a friend I would help. The money's good, and I've invested wisely, but it's time to let it go and keep exploring what I'm passionate about."

"That's a smart approach. We can't all make it straight out of the gate," Lola nodded. "I couldn't even begin to tell you all the jobs I had before settling here."

"This shop is great. Do you make all the art here?" Avery asked.

"Some of it. And I bring in local artists. I think it's important to showcase all the talent the island has to offer."

"These necklaces are stunning." Avery stopped in front of a few necklaces hanging from a driftwood hanger. One in particular caught her eye – a polished shell with a single pearl nestled inside, hanging from a delicate silver chain.

"My friend Prince makes them. He calls them mermaid shells." Lola winked at her and Avery felt her heart flutter.

"I'd love this one." She picked the necklace up.

"Here, try it on," Roman said, and moved to stand behind her. Lifting her hair, Avery shivered as his fingers brushed her skin, heat trailing from his touch, and felt the cool pendant settle between her breasts.

"How does it look?" Avery said, turning to find Roman hadn't moved. The moment drew out for a second as his eyes met hers, then trailed down to the pendant nestled at her chest.

"It's beautiful. Perfect for you… you look like a mermaid," Roman said.

Avery ducked her head, a smile flashing across her

face. "Thank you," she said, and stepped back, turning to examine a few handwoven bags. Picking up one that she knew Ruby would love, she wandered back to where Lola was finishing off the frame she was working on.

"I'd like to get this necklace and the bag, please."

"Actually, I'd like to buy the necklace for you." Roman stepped around Avery, and Lola beamed up at him.

"That's very nice of you. Do you want to wear it? It comes with a nice wooden box that's been carved in the shape of a shell as well."

"We'll take the box as it's quite pretty, but the lady can wear it if she'd like. I'd also like to buy the print up there," Roman said, and pointed to a large panoramic shot of the ocean. The photographer must have been standing in the water, because Avery could see both the brightly colored fish underwater and the palm trees and sand above it. It was a stunning shot. "Can I have it shipped?"

"Of course. I ship, but it'll take a few weeks," Lola said, and pulled out a pad to jot down his address. "This is a great piece; I'm sure you'll love it."

"It's for my mother. The most important woman in the world to me," Roman said. "She deserves to look at pretty things."

That was who he'd been talking to that one day, Avery realized as her fingers trailed over the necklace. Here she'd been half-convinced he had a girlfriend in the background, when all along he was just a mama's boy. Nothing wrong with that, Avery mused; family was just as important to her.

"Don't we all? Art is a great gift," Lola said, ringing him up and then quoting Avery for the price of the bag.

"This is for my sister," Avery said, knowing Ruby would love the bag.

"She'll love it," Lola promised. She waved goodbye to them as they left her shop.

"I didn't know you had a sister," Roman said.

Avery froze, looking at the back of his head as he rounded the Jeep. This was her moment to be honest with him – as a friend – that she wasn't who he thought she was. She opened her mouth to speak, then gasped as a fat raindrop hit her head.

"Uh oh," Roman called. "Get in! Cloudburst!"

Avery scampered to the Jeep just as the skies opened up, bucketing them with sheets of rain. Despite their best efforts, by the time it was done they were almost completely drenched, and laughing so hard that Avery had to wipe tears from her soaking wet face.

"I can't believe it's sunny again already," Avery gasped as Roman pulled away and drove to the road that would take them to the other side of the island. "What kind of rainstorm is that?"

"An island one," Roman laughed. "So much for putting the canvas on top to protect us."

"Well, it does protect from the sun." Avery laughed and looked down at her coverup clinging to her body. Looking at her new necklace, she ran a thumb over the pearl. "Thank you for my necklace. That was really sweet of you."

"Of course. I like knowing you'll have something from me," Roman said, then clamped his lips shut.

The silence stretched out between them as Avery pondered what he meant by that, then she shrieked when the radio blared music after they turned a curve in the road.

"That scared me," Avery laughed, her hand to her chest.

"Spotty island transmission." Roman chuckled, then shifted into a lower gear as they began a bumpy descent down a dirt path. Avery kept quiet and hung onto the roll bar, grateful for her seat belt as they jolted their way down the track to a small but pretty sand beach. Irma was right, Avery mused; this did look like its own tiny paradise. The water was calm, stretching like glass to the horizon.

"Ah, I see," Roman said, driving along the sand. "There's a wave break really far out, which essentially makes this a calm little pool of water."

"It's perfect," Avery decided.

"No, now it's perfect," Roman said, stopping the Jeep and looking at her. Avery met his eyes in confusion, and for a brief moment she thought he might kiss her. Then he said, "Look."

Turning, Avery saw that the cloudburst had moved out to sea, and the sun's rays hit the rain at the perfect angle to form a rainbow.

"Oh…" Avery breathed. "Yes, now it's perfect."

CHAPTER 30

"Since we're already wet, should we get in the water?" Roman asked, pulling out a bag of snorkel gear from the back of the Jeep. The sun was back out and the water was calm, barely a ripple marring the surface, and Avery tamped down on the anxiety that threatened to kick up. There couldn't be calmer swimming conditions, she reminded herself, and she used to love going in the water. Maybe now would be a good time to start working through the phobia she still carried from the accident.

"Sure, but you'll have to teach me to snorkel," Avery said, pulling her soaking wet coverup over her head and laying it across the hood of the Jeep to dry in the sun. Turning, she caught Roman looking at her simple emerald green sport bikini. Ruby had always rolled her eyes at this swimsuit, calling Avery 'Sporty Spice,' but Avery liked that it kept all her bits covered while allowing freedom of movement. No strings or ties to fuss with. She might as well have been wearing a sports bra. Avery could just see Ruby shaking her head now. She chuckled – she missed her sister deeply. She was looking forward to when she could get her phone back and communicate with the outside world again.

"Have you never snorkeled before?"

"Oh gosh, ages ago on the lake we used to go to in the summers. But there's not much to see in freshwater lakes." Avery laughed. "Just a few bluegills and a mucky bottom."

"I was lucky. I grew up close enough to the Florida Keys that we could go down for a weekend here and there. There's some good snorkeling in Key Largo if you can get out to the marine park. Up closer to shore is mucky though."

"Where did you grow up?"

"Ah, I was a trailer park kid." Roman shrugged, though Avery could sense an edge to his words. "Just Mom and me. She did the best she could, but we didn't have a lot. Those trips to Key Largo weren't often, but she'd certainly scrimped and saved so that we could do them."

"That's sweet of her. It sounds like she wanted to give you some nice memories," Avery said. Then she almost swallowed her tongue when Roman peeled off his t-shirt to reveal an actual eight-pack of muscles rippling down his chest. She'd known he was muscular, hadn't she? She'd been plastered all over his chest earlier in the week. But seeing it with her own two eyes was a whole different thing, and Avery found her mouth had gone dry.

"She really did," Roman said, placing his shirt next to hers and holding up a bottle of reef-safe sunscreen. "Have you applied?"

"Um, no, actually, I forgot," Avery admitted.

"Turn around. You'll fry with that pretty white skin of yours," Roman said.

Avery turned, trying to focus out on the horizon and not on the strong hands that were currently gently caressing her shoulders.

"I guess I always had a bit of a chip on my shoulder about being the poor kid at school," Roman continued, and Avery snapped back to attention. She was trying not to stretch and purr as his hands moved down her back. "Used to get in fights, that kind of stuff. Mom was getting worried. I had this one teacher, though – he saw potential in me, and put a camera in my hands. It was something I could channel all that pent-up angst into, you know?"

"Sure, I get it," Avery said, feeling a very different kind of pent-up angst building inside her.

"Pretty soon, I stopped caring about being the poor kid and started caring about finding beauty in the world through my lens. It started small, like trying to find beauty in the trailer park. I'd look for people who grew flowers on their stoop, or tended little herb gardens. That kind of thing. Slowly I started expanding my scope and began to explore the Everglades, which is where I really got hooked on the whole nature documentary thing. My first paid gig was producing a documentary on the pythons that swim in the Everglades. That was pretty intense."

"There are pythons there?"

"Sure are," Roman said. He handed the bottle to Avery over her shoulder. "Can you do mine now?"

"Oh, um, of course," Avery said, turning and staring at the broad expanse of his back. An intricate tattoo was etched across his shoulders, a stunning, almost tribal, design of a lion. For some reason, she hadn't been expecting him to be a tattoo guy, and couldn't help remarking on it.

"I like this," Avery said, tapping the lion.

"Thank you. It was to commemorate the first production I did for *National Geographic*. We were shooting to bring awareness to a conservancy for lions that had been abandoned by circuses. They couldn't go back to the wild, and needed to be retrained and homed in a safe place. There's this cool organization that takes care of them and teaches them how to lion again."

"How to lion again?" Avery laughed.

"You know... work in prides together. Hunt for food. Be outside. Be free, really. Well, as free as they can be. Luckily this place has acres of land for them to roam. It was really an incredible experience," Roman admitted. He turned when she tapped his back to let him know she was done.

"That's incredible. What an experience to have been a part of that." Avery smiled up at him. "That's something I'd like to do more of. I feel like I contribute on a small scale – through my job, for sure, with creating more environmentally friendly structures and practices. And I do my best at home and around our city to raise awareness with recycling and all that. But I'd love to learn more about getting involved with struggling animal populations and so on."

"I'd be happy to send you some information on a few of my favorite organizations," Roman said. "Maybe someday you'll visit them."

"I think I'd like that," Avery said, "But really, what a dichotomy between producing a reality show and covering abused lions. How do you... I don't know..."

"How do I live with myself?" Roman laughed, running a hand through his hair.

"No, not that. I mean you could be doing a lot worse, like filming those girls-gone-wild tapes or something."

"Yeah, no thanks," Roman said with a laugh. They wandered down the beach, giving their sunscreen time to soak in. "I think – well, you want me to be honest?"

"Sure, go for it," Avery said.

"I think I'll probably always have a bit of that poor kid living inside me. I know what it feels like to go without. I know what it feels like to be hungry. I know what it is to eat canned beans – if we were lucky, that is – or survive on a bag of rice and dried lentils for weeks at a time. My mom always added spices and flavors and made things fun, but I wasn't dumb. I knew we barely got by. The one time we ate out for dinner? On my graduation from high school. I don't think I've ever seen her more proud of me. We went to Applebee's and I had a steak. I've eaten much better steaks since then, but I'll tell you what – that Applebee's steak? The best thing I've ever tasted."

"Where's your mom now?" Avery asked, touched by the story.

"I put her up in a lovely little two-bedroom house just off the water. She refused waterfront – said it was too fancy – but she likes the house. I wanted to get her something bigger and nicer, but she said she didn't want to clean anything bigger. She's happy as can be. Has a couple neighbors she plays mah jong with, a little dog she walks every night, and her very own vegetable garden. I would produce a thousand more reality shows if it meant I could keep her happy like that. Luckily I don't need to, but I would."

"You're a good man, Roman. It sounds like your mother raised you right," Avery said.

Roman laughed. "Well, she'll tell you a few stories about my more troublesome years. But we all have those, right?"

"Erm…some of us." Avery shrugged a shoulder.

Roman's mouth dropped open. "Don't tell me you never got into trouble!"

"I mean… like, what counts as trouble?"

"Drinking? Smoking pot? Making out in the back-seat of a car with the quarterback? Breaking curfew? Taking your parents' car out for a test drive?" Avery kept shaking her head no until Roman threw up his hands.

"Woman! You need to live a little."

"I did return a library book three weeks late one time." Avery pretended to hang her head in shame.

Roman groaned. "Well, now, I see we've got some making up to do," Roman decided.

Avery hesitated before continuing to walk into the water. "I don't want to get into trouble in the water, please," Avery said, her voice stiff. Roman paused, studying her.

"That's fine; I can respect that. How about we spend some time testing out the snorkel masks in the shallows for a little bit then?" he asked, his eyes on hers. He'd left his sunglasses on the shore and she could read the questions he had. She just wasn't ready to answer them.

"Perfect," Avery said, then surprised him by kicking a spray of water at him. She laughed at the shock on his face. "Okay, see? I can be a little trouble."

Avery's heart skipped a beat as he picked her up and threw her over his shoulder, running until they were waist-deep in the water.

"I should toss you right in," Roman threatened.

"Please don't," Avery begged, half laughing, half worried, trying to force the panic down.

"You're lucky I'm a gentleman," Roman said, and let her slide down his body, every last inch of her grazing his skin. She narrowed her eyes up at him.

"Not that much of a gentleman."

"Well, you know, a work in progress." Roman grinned. "Now, masks. You'll probably want to pull your hair back. Snorkel goes on the right. To start we aren't even going to swim – we'll just put the mask on, bend at the waist, and put our faces in the water. You can work on breathing through the snorkel, and if it freaks you out, just stand up. Easy, okay?"

"Right, got it," Avery said, repeating over and over to herself that she was fine, this was no big deal, and she could stand up at any moment. Placing the mask on her face, she tightened the strap and put the mouthpiece of the snorkel in her mouth. Bending over, Avery put her face in the water. She giggled when she saw a tiny silver fish darting by her toes. Otherwise, there was nothing to see other than that she needed to touch up her pedicure. It was hard to be panicked, Avery realized, when she was in three feet of crystal-clear water, with the sun on her back, a muscular guy at her side, and all the time in her day to ease into snorkeling.

Standing up, she looked at Roman as he stood up as well. She burst out laughing, the snorkel dropping from her mouth.

"You look ridiculous," Avery said.

"Oh? You think you're looking all sexy with a mask on? Because you look just as ridiculous," Roman teased.

Avery laughed again. "Okay, got it. Snorkel masks are not the most flattering."

"Nope. How'd it go, though? You want to try floating? I'll stand next to you while you do it."

"Just float? Face down and breathe?"

"Yup, saltwater is extra buoyant. So long as you breathe, you'll float just fine along the top," Roman promised. Avery nodded, and he said, "I'll be standing right here in case you have any issues. Promise."

"Thank you, sorry for being nervous."

"Don't apologize. We all have our things. I think people who make fun of others who are trying something out of their comfort zones are assholes."

Avery wondered if that went back to his days of being bullied and getting in fights. Putting the snorkel back in her mouth, she bent at the waist and put her face in the water. Once she was comfortable with her breathing again, she kicked her legs up so that she floated in a straight horizontal line in the water. Although her feet leaving the ground made her stomach flip in a nervous little knot at first, she forced herself to breathe slowly. She soon realized that everything was fine, and she could just stand up again when she felt like it. Putting her feet in the sand, she lifted her head.

"I think I'm ready," Avery said.

"Great, you're doing wonderful," Roman assured her. "But maybe just hold my hand in case."

Not saying anything, Avery dipped her face back in the water, and when Roman reached out for her hand, she let him take it. Together they kicked lazily through the water. Well, Roman kicked and basically just tugged Avery after him, but she found herself enjoying it and relaxing bit by bit. When a huge school of blue tangs swam past them, she was able to smile at them through her mask and not freak out and run away. She prided herself on working through her fear, but a few minutes later she froze when she saw a large silver fish circling her. Almost as long as her, with tiger stripes down its side, the fish had a menacing jaw filled with jagged teeth and Avery could have sworn it was eying her up. Gasping, she went to put her feet on the ground and stand up, wanting to shoo the scary fish away.

When her feet didn't reach the ground, Avery realized how far out they were. It only took an instant for panic to race through her, choking her throat as she flailed, the snorkel falling from her mouth. Opening her mouth to scream, she gulped a huge amount of sea water and coughed, sputtering as her head went under the water.

Muscular arms circled her, dragging her to the surface and spiriting her quickly toward shore. Avery clung to Roman, her eyes wide in panic, as she choked out the water she'd swallowed, sputtering and trying to take a breath.

"Shhh, just in through the nose, out through the mouth. Slow breaths," Roman said, dropping to his knees in the sand and placing her on the ground. "Slow even breaths. On my count… one, two, three… and out again." He ran his hand in circular motions on her back, soothing her as the panic slowed, until she could take a normal breath.

Tears welled in her eyes and Avery dropped her face to her hands.

"I'm so embarrassed."

CHAPTER 31

"*D*on't be. Let's walk through what happened out there," Roman said, sitting down in the sand beside her. "I find it helps take some of the scary stuff away if you talk through it right away."

"There was a big fish. With nasty-looking teeth. He was eyeing me up like I was dinner. I was just going to stand up and shoo him away, since I know he's probably more scared of me, but then my feet didn't reach the ground and I realized how far out we were."

"Barracuda," Roman said, and reached out to touch the pendant at her chest, "I forgot to tell you to take off your necklace when you were snorkeling. He probably wasn't looking to bite you, but rather the necklace. It looks like a lure to them."

"Shut up. I was wearing a fishing lure on my neck?" Avery looked askance at her necklace.

"Pretty much. Best not to wear jewelry in the ocean. So was it the barracuda or the depth that scared you?"

"The depth."

"Why?"

"I thought I could stand there and I couldn't."

"Didn't you say you were a strong swimmer?"

"I am."

"What happened to make you afraid of the water?" Roman asked, accurately surmising that there was much more to her fear than just what had happened out there.

"So... I've never been the biggest risk taker," Avery began, pushing the wet hair from her face.

"Here, come on, let's get in the shade and dried off. It sounds like a glass of wine may help?"

"Yeah, it will," Avery said, and stood on shaky feet. Roman kept an eye on her as he laid out a beach blanket on the sand and pulled the cooler and hamper from the Jeep. Ushering her over, he pointed to the blanket.

"Sit."

"Yes, sir," Avery said, plopping onto the blanket. He handed her a towel and she wrapped it around her, grateful for the coverage.

"Talk," Roman said, handing her a glass of white wine that he had poured. She took a sip, the cool liquid soothing her throat.

"As I said, I'm not much of a risk-taker. I was dating an outdoorsy adventure type – you know, all, Woooohoooo! Let's jump from planes! and all that. Everything for him was an adventure. Frankly, he was a little exhausting, but still, it was fun to try new things and sort of open up a different way of living."

"Sure, I get that," Roman said, unpacking the hamper as she talked.

"Anyway, he took me kayaking on a river. Without telling me there were rapids. Like… big rapids. He thought it would be funny to see my shock."

"That's just… wow, that's really dangerous." Roman looked at her in shock.

"Yeah, like expert level rapids. I shouldn't have been on that river. I… well, I died that day," Avery said. She took another sip of wine and stared out at the water. Not only had she actually died that day, but it seemed like a part of her spirit had died along with her.

"Avery, I'm so sorry," Roman said, reaching out to grab her hand. He squeezed it for a moment and said nothing else, letting her speak at her own pace. She appreciated that about him.

"The kayak flipped… yadda yadda. Basically, I had to be revived and then was in a medically-induced coma for a week. After that… It took a long time to recover from my injuries."

"That's terrifying."

"It was, yeah."

"And the boyfriend?"

"Took off as soon as I came out of the coma. I'm not sure if he wasn't ready to face what a negligent asshole he'd been, or if he just wasn't capable of helping me recover. I wasn't exactly a fun girlfriend there for a while." Avery shrugged.

Roman shocked her by letting out a string of obscenities. "Being in a relationship isn't always about being there for the fun times. What kind of jerk leaves his woman in a hospital bed? What an incompetent stupid asshole. I'm sorry, Avery, but you're better off without him," Roman fumed.

"Yes, well, I see that now," Avery admitted, hugging her arms around her knees. "It just stung for a bit. Like, made me feel not all that worthwhile. If he could only stay with me when I was whole... you know?"

"Not all men are assholes. Sounds like he was incredibly immature."

"I know that. I know all of it. Rationally I know all the things, but the water thing still kind of gets me."

"I don't doubt it. Drowning will do that to a person," Roman said.

Avery was shocked to feel a giggle bubble up. "You're absolutely right. Drowning *will* do that to a person."

"Well, I think you're pretty brave for going back in the water."

She smiled at him gratefully. "Thank you. I don't particularly feel that brave, especially not after gulping a gallon of sea water, but still. It's nice to hear. Even coming down here was a huge step for me."

"Have you dated since your accident?" Roman asked.

"Nope. Hid myself under a rock and worked my way up the career ladder," Avery admitted.

"Hence the part about you not getting any in a couple years?" Roman asked, then laughed at the look of shock on Avery's face.

"Roman!" she shrieked, and smacked him lightly on the arm. "You weren't supposed to eavesdrop!"

"It's not like you all were talking that quietly. I was just walking down the hallway."

"My mortification is complete," Avery decided, burying her face in her hands.

"Nothing to be ashamed of," Roman promised. "I've gone a long time in the past before, too. But, you know, should you want to change that..."

It was meant to be a joking comment, but the silence stretched out between them as Avery looked over at him, her eyes huge in her face. Reading her correctly, Roman came and crouched in front of her, his face inches from hers.

"Are you telling me you want to change that?"

"I... Roman..." Avery looked helplessly at him. "This is weird. I'm on a dating show –"

"Do you like him?" Roman whispered.

Avery shook her head no. "But it wouldn't speak well of my character if I didn't give it an honest shot," Avery whispered back, though it pained her to say the words.

"I think about you, Avery. A lot. More than I would like," Roman said. Reaching out, he brushed his thumb across her lips.

"It's a tough time. I don't know what to do."

"What do you want to do?"

"I want to kiss you," Avery said, knowing her cheeks were probably flaming, and not caring.

"Then why don't you?"

"Because I don't like muddy waters. And this whole show thing is very muddied water," Avery admitted. "I'm not a liar or a sneak, and I'm certainly not savvy enough to juggle two men. I... can you wait?"

"Wait to see how your date with Beckett goes? Wait to see if he chooses you? Now, what kind of man would that make me?" Roman asked, frustration lacing his voice as he sat back on his heels.

"And what kind of woman would it make me if I dated two men at once?" Avery whispered.

"Ugh." Roman let out a sound of frustration, then wiped his hand across his face. "I hate to say this, but you're right. And I did promise you this would be just friends today. So I'll stand by my word – but promise me one thing."

"What's that?"

"When this is over, no matter how it ends, you'll give me one date. One actual real date where we can give this an honest chance. If you haven't fallen head over heels in love with Beckett, that is."

"I don't think that'll happen." Avery smiled and felt the tension ease from her shoulders. "But yes, I'll give you that promise."

"Fair enough. In that case, may I interest you in a sampling of cheeses?" Roman brandished a plate of cheese under her nose and Avery found herself giggling again.

"Why yes, you may. I love nothing more than cheese on the beach with a friend."

"For now," Roman promised.

CHAPTER 32

It felt weird, sleeping alone in their room that night, and Avery wondered if Cherylynn had made her move on Beckett or not. What would it say about him if he made a move on her the next night, or whenever they had their date? Was he just going to sample all the women and then decide which flavor he liked best? Avery was struggling to wrap her head around how that worked, and it just really didn't sit well with her.

She could leave, she thought, turning and punching her pillow under her shoulder more. She could just get up and leave and quit the show.

And be with Roman.

The thought of being with Roman was really what was keeping her up, if she were to be honest with herself – which wasn't always a fun thing to do. But she couldn't stop thinking about him and their almost-kiss. How could she be falling for another man when she was supposed to be focused on Beckett? What kind of weird alternate universe had she landed herself in? She wished she had her phone so she could talk this out with Ruby, but that wasn't an option right now. Sighing, she resigned herself to a long night of lying awake.

Avery blinked awake, the sun in her eyes, and took a moment to register what had woken her. The gong below sounded again – it was their fifteen-minute warning before filming. Shoot! She must have fallen asleep late into the night after all, and overslept this morning.

Scrambling, Avery shoved her messy hair into a high ponytail, took the world's fastest shower, and brushed her teeth. Throwing on a pair of cut-off shorts and a breezy red tank top, she zipped downstairs just as Jack stepped onto the pool deck. Beckett stood next to him, and Cherylynn was back, standing next to Lisette in the clothes she'd worn the day before. Avery craned her neck to try and catch Cherylynn's eye, but she just looked straight ahead.

Hmmm. Avery wondered what was up there. Casting an eye back at the coffee station, she snapped back to attention when Jack began to speak.

"Good morning, ladies. I trust you all made good use of your downtime yesterday?" The women all nodded; Avery wondered what they'd all done, or if any of them had seen her ride off with Roman. In retrospect, it probably hadn't looked that good to be leaving the villa with him.

"Avery," Jack said, and she realized that he had already said her name twice.

"Yes, I'm sorry," Avery said, a sheepish smile on her face.

"Beckett would like to take you on a date next. Can you be ready to leave in about thirty minutes?"

"Of course," Avery said, and then remembered she was supposed to be smiling, not looking worried about the upcoming date.

"Lovely. Meet in front in thirty minutes. The rest of you, enjoy your time in paradise," Jack said, beaming his too-white smile at them. Beckett wiggled his eyebrows at Avery. She grinned – while mentally cringing – and went back up the stairs, trying to figure out what to pack for her day out. Remembering Ruby's advice about layers, she kept the outfit she had on and packed a few more things. Taking a few moments to tame her hair, she waited in the room until the last possible moment, hoping Cherylynn would come upstairs and tell her about her date, or what to expect. When her friend didn't arrive, Avery had no choice but to descend the deathtrap stairs and meet Beckett, who was waiting at the front door.

"Ready for our big day out, baby?" Beckett asked, grinning at her and throwing an arm around her shoulder. Avery cringed at his familiarity, but forced a smile for the cameras as they climbed into the van outside.

"What are the plans for the day?"

"Oh, I've got something great planned, don't you worry," Beckett promised. He began chattering away about surfing and how he wished the island had bigger waves so he could show off his moves. Avery just stared at him, and finally nodded along, learning quickly that she didn't have to say much for him to just keep talking. And talking. And talking.

When the van finally rolled to a stop, Avery glanced out of the window.

"Azure Falls Hotel?"

"Yeah, baby, they got a lazy river and a DJ. We're gonna party all day. It'll be sick," Beckett promised as he helped her from the van.

Avery pasted a smile on her face and walked with him through the lobby, cringing a little as people turned their heads to stare at the cameraman following them. Beckett seemed to enjoy the attention, and smiled and nodded at everyone like he was a famous movie star. They were quickly ushered to a VIP section where a cabana bed was set up by the pool. Even though it was only mid-day, a bottle of champagne chilled in a bucket by the bed, and a waiter stood by at the ready.

"Welcome to Azure Falls. We're here for anything you need today, please don't hesitate to ask." The waiter smiled, and Avery took the opportunity to order a large coffee and a croissant. She'd need the caffeine to get through this day, she thought.

"How about a mimosa instead?" Beckett asked, popping the bottle and laughing as the cork sailed into the pool, narrowly missing a woman swimming there.

"Mmm, not quite yet. I want coffee first," Avery said and sat down on the bed.

"Oh, the DJ's starting already. Sweet," Beckett said, and stood by the side of the pool. When the DJ began playing an easygoing beat, Beckett whooped and fist-pumped the air.

Did this guy have no idea how out of line he was? It wasn't like this was a party place. Avery looked around at the families staring at Beckett like he was nuts. The DJ was playing a super mellow reggae song, which was absolutely fitting with the relaxed vibe of the pool. Clearly Beckett had no sense of his surroundings. Or maybe he just didn't care.

"Beckett," Avery called, patting the bed beside her, "why don't you come sit down?"

"Sure thing, baby-cakes." Beckett laughed and dove onto the bed, leaning on one elbow and trailing a finger down her back, making Avery cringe. "I like a woman who wants me in bed."

Great, Avery thought. It's going to be a long day.

"Why don't you tell me about yourself, Beckett? How long have you lived in California?" Seeing that his glass was already empty, she figured out her strategy pretty quickly. Keep his glass full, keep him talking about himself, and – somehow – get through what was already shaping up to be a nightmare of a day.

Two hours and two bottles later, Beckett was snoring soundly in the daybed, much to everyone's relief. He'd treated the crowd to a rendition of "One Love," had pretended to ride an imaginary pony, and had cannon-balled into the pool enough times that the manager had finally had to have a quiet word with him. Avery had intervened at that point, dragging him back to the daybed, feeding him French fries and water until he'd finally passed out – hopefully for a long time, Avery thought.

Pulling her book from her bag, she commenced to have a lovely afternoon, catching up on a few chapters and sampling a lovely fruit salad from the kitchen.

"Hey, baby! Oh man, what a great nap. I have to take a leak. I'll be back." Beckett woke up at full speed, startling Avery, and was gone before she could say anything else. Taking a deep breath, she put her book away and steeled herself for what came next.

"I'm hungry. Are you ready for our dinner? I have something special planned," Beckett promised, smiling at her from the end of the cabana. He was handsome, Avery would give him that, but the idea of spending the night with him was proving to be increasingly difficult to swallow.

"What's that?"

"We have a suite upstairs that we can go change in. Then I've got a romantic dinner planned." Beckett offered her his arm and Avery took it. What else could she do?

"That sounds lovely, Beckett. Is it a restaurant in town? I've been hoping to try out some of the local places."

"It's a surprise, Avery." Beckett grinned and punched the button for the elevator. It was incredibly awkward to ride up in an elevator with a cameraman standing behind them, Avery realized. She stared straight ahead at the door, not sure what to say.

"Here we are!" Beckett proclaimed, throwing open the door to the penthouse. Rose petals were scattered everywhere – through the sitting room and into the bedroom, where Avery could see them on the bed, which had candles lit around it. Her stomach flipped and a trickle of sweat dripped down her neck. How was she going to handle this situation? It was incredibly presumptuous of Beckett to even assume she would be willing to go into a bedroom with him, let alone to spread rose petals everywhere.

"Pretty, right?" Beckett said, oblivious to Avery's panic, and grabbed her arm, tugging her toward the balcony. "And here's the surprise!"

A table for two was set on the balcony, with roses in a crystal vase, a bottle of champagne chilling in a bucket, and the view of the ocean and the setting sun in front of them. It was stunningly pretty, and absolutely wrong.

"Bathroom's through there if you want to change. I took the liberty of ordering for us, so food should be here shortly."

"Thanks," Avery said, and stole away to the bathroom. There, she braced her arms on the sink and stared at herself in the mirror. What was she even doing here? She should just leave. Could she? Would it make her look like a fool on television? There was nothing in the contract that said she had to engage in sexual relations with this man. She could very easily say no, Avery reminded herself; they just set this all up for the drama of it all. Taking a deep breath, she dug into her pack and changed into a simple cotton dress with pink flowers splashed across it. Fussing with her hair just a bit, she grimaced into the mirror.

"Let's get this over with," Avery muttered, and went out to meet Beckett.

"You look pretty," Beckett said from where he sat, covered food dishes already on the table.

"Thank you. You look handsome as well," Avery said.

"So I've heard." Beckett tossed his hair, putting on a show, but Avery caught something in his eyes. Taking a deep breath, she leaned across the table and put her hand on his.

"Beckett?"

"Yes?"

"Cut the 'cool bro' act. It's not working with me. You can just be you," Avery said. She knew she was taking a risk that he would get angry with her.

Confusion crossed his face – then relief dawned.

"Really?"

"Really. It's a little obnoxious, if I'm being honest."

"Ugh, I thought it might be." Beckett rubbed a hand over his face. "Honestly, it feels so weird to be on camera that I've been putting on a show."

"Well, knock it off. I was embarrassed to be with you today."

"I could tell. That's why I drank a lot and passed out. I was kind of embarrassed for myself."

"Just... just be normal. Tell me who you really are and go from there."

Avery breathed a sigh of relief as the tension left Beckett's shoulders, and he became much more relaxed and engaging. Despite her initial misgivings, she found herself laughing over dinner and enjoying their conversation. He was surprisingly smart, and had a knack for helping the kids at his camp break through their own barriers. By the end of dinner, she realized that Beckett suffered from social anxiety, and tried to mask it by putting on a show.

"Why come on this show then?" Avery asked.

"I wanted to try something new. And hey, the publicity is good for the camp," Beckett admitted. They'd moved inside and were sitting companionably on the couch. Avery had even forgotten the cameraman was there, but perhaps the glass of champagne she'd had at dinner had helped with that.

"That makes sense," Avery smiled up at him. A moment later, she was surprised to find his lips suddenly pressed against hers while he pressed her back into the couch.

She decided to give it a moment, because she really did want to give this an honest chance. She let Beckett kiss her to see if she had any feelings at all for him, but when nothing fluttered in her stomach and no pangs of lust ripped through her, she gently pressed against his chest, pushing him back.

"Thank you," Avery said, nudging him further back on the couch.

"I think we could go explore a little further, no?" Beckett stood up and looked down at her, holding out his hand. Just then, Avery caught a glimpse of movement over his shoulder, and realized that Roman had been in the room all along. His face, disgust raging across it, said all it needed to say before he slipped from the room.

"And I think we have a better use for our time." Avery smiled up at him, though her heart had sunk in her chest. "Have you ever played cribbage before?"

"Seriously? I love cribbage," Beckett exclaimed, plopping down on the couch next to her.

"I think we can be friends then, Beckett."

CHAPTER 33

"Well?" Cherylynn demanded the next morning when they finally returned to the villa. Nothing had happened between them, and once the pressure of a romance had been taken off the table, Avery had found herself enjoying Beckett's company. He was kind of like a dopey big brother, she'd realized, and she had enjoyed teasing him about his antics earlier in the day.

"Well, what?" Avery asked, dropping her bag on the bed.

"Did you sleep with him?" Cherylynn demanded.

Avery caught a look in her eye. "Oh, hon. You really like him, don't you?" she asked.

"Not if he's sleeping with all the women here," Cherylynn swore, her face mutinous.

"I did not sleep with him," Avery promised. "He's not for me. We played cribbage and talked about our lives. He's a friend, Cherylynn, and that's all he'll be."

"So… you're leaving then?"

"I don't know what happens next. Do you just leave if you know it's not right?"

"I want to tell you yes, please leave. Because I like him and there's a lot of money on the table. But I also promised to be your friend, no matter what." Cherylynn took a deep breath. "So I'll tell you to stay and play this hand out. I know the money can change your life."

"It could change yours, too."

"I don't have debts like you do, hon. Just play it out. But don't sleep with him, okay? I think we could have something after this is all done."

"Not going to be a problem. Plus, I don't think we'd even get a chance to. There's just a couple more dates and then one more challenge, right?"

"Right. So, in the meantime, let's hang by the pool and chat about girl stuff and pretend we don't have a care in the world, right? Never let them see you sweat," Cherylynn said.

What Avery really wanted to do was find Roman and explain to him about the kiss, but he somehow successfully managed to avoid her over the next couple of days while they waited out the other women's overnight dates. She wondered if he had gone off to oversee the production of the dates, or if he was actually avoiding her. Either way, the tension was building up inside her.

"Would you stop looking for him?" Cherylynn said. "Play it cool."

"I'm not looking for him," Avery hissed.

"Liar."

"Just shut up."

They were back at the pool deck, ready for their last challenge.

"Welcome back, everyone. I trust you've enjoyed your one-on-one time with Beckett?" The women clapped, but Avery could tell the tension in the room had changed. "For our last challenge, we actually have a race. The winner gets a two-week stay at the Laughing Mermaid, here on Siren Island." This time the cheers from the women were real.

"Please meet down at the beach in five minutes, and we'll get started."

"Uh-oh," Avery muttered, not liking the sound of a race that started by the water. Hoping against hope it had nothing to do with the water, she trudged after the other girls. Sara waved goodbye to them from the pool, her face sad – with her bad ankle, there was no way she could participate in a race.

A row of ocean kayaks greeted them when they turned the corner, and Avery's heart dropped.

"I can't do this," Avery whispered to Cherylynn, turning in a full circle to look for Roman. He must know she wouldn't be able to do this. But he was nowhere to be found. The other producer was standing by a palm tree.

"It's pretty simple, ladies. Beckett is around that point, waiting for you. The first woman to reach him, wins," Jack said, pointing to a spot where the island curved and the cliffs jutted out from the water.

It looked an impossible distance away. Avery grimaced as waves smashed against the rocks, and she felt sweat trickle down her back.

"What do you want to do, Avery? I've got your back," Cherylynn promised.

"I… I don't know," Avery whispered.

"You do not have to go out there. No show is worth it. You have a choice," Cherylynn said, facing her.

"I know. But if I don't do this… will I always wonder if I could've? What if this breaks me free from my fear?"

"It might," Cherylynn said, though she didn't look too convinced.

"I'm doing it," Avery decided, ignoring the anxiety that ate at her gut.

"You sure?" Cherylynn raised an eyebrow.

"Yes. Stop asking me before I chicken out."

"There's no life jackets," Cherylynn pointed out.

"I can swim," Avery reminded her.

"Fine, but try not to go too fast. I'll stay by you."

"I'm going as fast as I can, to get this over with."

"All righty, but if one of us wins we promise to share it with the other, right?"

"Oh my gosh, yes. That would be so fun," Avery said, distracted from her panic for a moment by the thought of a two-week girls' trip at Irma's place.

"Saddle up, lady. Let's ride," Cherylynn said, and climbed into her kayak. There were spotters there, helping them out into the water, and Avery gingerly climbed into the seat of the kayak, then took the paddle that was handed to her. She gulped as a wave slapped against the hull, trying to tamp down on the nausea that rose in her throat while the spotter guided her kayak out into the depths.

"Ready? Set? Go!" Jack cried from the shore, and Avery began blindly paddling as fast as she could, panic surging her forward. The sooner she finished this race, the sooner she was off the boat. Paddle, paddle, paddle. Avery repeated the words over and over in her head, her eyes focused on the tip of her kayak, zoning out everything else around her.

She didn't hear Cherylynn's cries telling her to wait. She didn't hear the spotters shout, telling her to turn her kayak into the waves instead of horizontal to them. The last thing she saw before the wave overtook her was Roman on a kayak, fear on his face, paddling as fast as he could for her.

Panic engulfed her and she choked on the water, confused on which way to swim. Kicking out, she didn't realize she was moving away from the surface until little dots began to spot her eyes, and a haze drifted over her mind.

CHAPTER 34

*L*ips pressed to hers, and Avery's eyes popped open. Even in the sting of saltwater she could see... was it fins? Pulling back, she cried out, taking in more water as Jolie and Mirra circled her, impossibly enchanting, their tails glistening in the sun as they took turns breathing life into Avery.

"But... you're mermaids," Avery said into the water, and Mirra shook her head, pressing her lips to Avery's once more, filling her with the breath of life. It was as if she sucked the water from Avery's lungs, and filled her with light and magic.

"Don't talk, Avery. You're still underwater," Jolie chided her, pulling her toward where the light of the sun beckoned from the surface. Avery wondered how she could hear her, then, or if she was hallucinating.

"Go to him. The one you trust. The one who loves you," Mirra said, pushing her toward the light.

Avery broke the surface and took a massive breath,

looking wildly around. Beckett raced in circles in his kayak, and two empty kayaks floated in the waves. Avery couldn't speak – she could barely keep her head above water – but she idly wondered who the other kayak belonged to. When Roman's head broke the surface, realization dawned. He was diving for her.

Without thinking, Avery swam harder than she'd ever swum before, completely focused on Roman. He was safe, that was all she knew, and she had to get to him.

"She's there!" Cherylynn screamed.

Beckett turned his kayak toward her, but she kept swimming, not caring about the cameras or anything except getting to Roman. He'd turned at Cherylynn's shout, and met her in the water, wrapping his arms around her and hauling her back to his kayak.

"I didn't sleep with him. I let him kiss me," Avery babbled. "I'm so sorry I let him kiss me. I just had to know that there were no feelings."

"Shhh, Avery, shhh," Roman said, holding the kayak with one arm and Avery with the other.

"No, you need to know it. I couldn't find you. I had to tell you and I couldn't find you. I thought you hated me."

"I know you didn't sleep with him, Avery. I review the tapes, remember? Now hush. He's coming," Roman said, his arm tight around her waist. In moments, Beckett was there, hauling her on board his kayak.

"Hey now, that was a silly thing to do," Beckett said, teasing her, but she could see the worry on his face.

"I'm sorry. I shouldn't have gone out on the kayak."

"And everyone should have had life jackets," Roman said, his face furious as he began to swim his kayak to shore. Avery watched as he berated his production assistant, but she had to wonder – why had he not warned her about this challenge? He knew what her fears were.

"Well, now, that was some excitement, hey?" Beckett said as the kayak bumped the sand.

Roman came over, hauling Avery from the kayak and slinging her up in his arms to carry her.

"Does this mean nobody wins?" Georgette called from her kayak, and even Beckett turned and glared at her. "Sorry, just asking."

"Nobody wins. Elimination tonight."

And that, it seemed, was that, Avery thought. She dropped her head onto Roman's shoulder and let him carry her back to the villa. It was over and she could go home and start her life over. There was nothing else to be done, nothing else to fake, and she'd done enough to push herself far outside her comfort zone.

One thing was for certain, though: She'd never be getting on a kayak again in her life.

Avery slept for the next few hours, the adrenaline crash from her experience completely wiping her out. Cherylynn nudged her awake later in the day.

"Hey, we've got about an hour before the final ceremony. I brought you some food." She held out a plate of fruit and croissants.

Avery sat up in bed, leaning against the headboard,

and took the food gratefully. "I shouldn't have gone out. I don't know what I was trying to prove," she admitted.

"You took off like a speed demon. I don't know what you were doing, but you were flying. You would have been fine if you'd turned your kayak into the waves, but you didn't. You really scared me, Avery. You were down there a long time," Cherylynn said, her eyes filling with tears.

"I know. I'm sorry. I was stupid. I really was. I think I was so determined to try and overcome this fear. I don't know why... maybe I was doing, like, shock therapy to make me not so scared anymore? It wasn't smart. It really wasn't."

"How's that fear of yours now?"

"Well, let's just say I won't be planning any kayaking trips in the future. But oddly enough, I'm not so scared of the water anymore. There are some pretty beautiful things out there. I think... yeah, I think I'll explore it more. Slowly and in my own time, but I will."

"Well, I'd call that a win then, right? I mean, it's baby steps, but that's still a huge win. Because, let's be honest, you can spend your whole life avoiding getting on a kayak just fine. But being in water? That's a lot harder to dance around. I'm glad you're not so scared of it anymore, though I think you took about ten years off my life when you went overboard."

"You ready for tonight?" Avery asked, wanting to change the subject. She wasn't ready to tell anyone about the mermaids. It was a secret given to her, and she wanted to keep it close to her heart, taking it out to examine it when she had time to breathe again.

"I'm nervous. What if he doesn't choose me?"

"Honestly, I'm not sure he'll pick any of us." Avery shrugged.

"He has to pick. Or nobody wins the money."

"Well, I don't know what will happen. I think I'm ready for it to be over, though. This has been one strange experience for me, that's for sure."

"Well, you definitely got out of your comfort zone."

"Indeed. Okay, let's do the dance one more time."

A half hour later they stood, for the last time, on the pool deck. Music played softly in the background, and the flames of the torches flickered in the twilight breezes. Everyone was there, including Irma, Jolie, and Mirra. Avery wanted desperately to run over to them and thank them for their help, but Jack started the ceremony as soon as they came out.

"Good evening, everyone, and we are ready to start the final ceremony in *Swept Away*," Jack intoned. Avery wondered if he'd been hitting the bottle. "While it's been an eventful day, it looks like you're none the worse for wear, Avery?"

"I'm doing just fine, thanks." She smiled politely.

"Lovely to hear. Wouldn't do to have anyone die on us." Jack laughed while the rest of them looked at him like he was crazy. Yup, he'd definitely had a few cocktails this afternoon, Avery thought. "Now, Beckett, it's time for you to choose your lovely lady, your partner in crime, your… everything!"

"Okay, Jack," Beckett said, stepping forward and nudging the man back. "I'll take it from here. Ladies, first of all, I'd like to say what a pleasure it has been to meet you all. I really enjoyed getting to know each and every one of you, and I am honored to have you all be a part of my story."

Laying it on a little thick, Avery thought, and almost rolled her eyes.

"But since I must choose only one woman, I will go with my heart."

Silence settled over the group and they all waited as Beckett drew the moment out.

"Avery, I choose you."

CHAPTER 35

"Why did you really choose me, Beckett?"

It was the day after the final elimination ceremony. There had been tears, anger, and more drama than Avery had been expecting. Cherylynn, true to her word, had hugged Avery and promised to be in touch.

"I just need to lick my wounds a little first, you understand?" Cherylynn had whispered in Avery's ear when she'd hugged her goodbye. Avery did understand, and admired the fact that Cherylynn hadn't turned on her for winning the prize. It said a lot about her as a person, in Avery's estimation.

"I wanted to share this prize with a friend," Beckett admitted, stretching his legs out in front of him. They had claimed two of the lounge chairs by the now-empty pool deck, watching as the post-production crew dismantled cameras from the house and did general clean-up.

"But what about love?" Avery asked.

"What about it?" Beckett turned to look at Avery. "I don't love any of these women. And I don't think anyone is under any illusions that I do. Even production isn't. This is 'reality' TV – I gave them what they wanted, and I'm being paid handsomely to do so. So are you."

"That's a lot of money to not at least try," Avery said, the win still weighing uncomfortably on her.

"I did try. Why do you think I kicked all those catty women off? I gave everyone some time. And I do think I found someone I'd like to spend more time with."

"Who?" Avery asked, lowering her sunglasses and meeting his eyes.

"Promise you won't be offended?"

"Promise."

"Well, obviously I want to see you again, because you're my friend now. But I kind of like Cherylynn."

"Did you tell her that?"

"No, but I will. I have her contact information, and I think I'll stop by this ranch of hers on the way back to California."

"She would love that. I think she really likes you, Beckett."

"I really like her, too."

"Then why in the world didn't you pick her? This makes no sense to me."

"Because I don't want to spend the rest of our relationship wondering if she just chose me for the money,"

Beckett said, running a hand through his hair. "I don't want to put that kind of pressure on us."

"I do see. But that could have also been an amazing gift to each other."

"She doesn't need the money, Avery. Didn't she tell you about that ranch of hers?"

"Yes, but I'm sure the money could help with a few things around the ranch."

"Cherylynn's *loaded*, Avery. It's not some dilapidated ranch with falling-down stables. There's oil on their land. And she's part owner. Money is not something she needs from me. If anything, she's more successful than I am. Taking this game show and prize out of the mix will give me a better understanding of who she is, and what she wants from a partner."

"I had no idea," Avery said, shocked that the easy-going Cherylynn was wealthy. "She's gonna give you hell though for putting her through this."

"I look forward to it. At least I'll know she cares."

"Tell her hi from me when you go," Avery said, reaching out to pat his arm. "I'm glad we met, Beckett. This was a tough experience, but a good one for me."

"I think so. But you've got your own angry person to deal with. At least judging from his face." Beckett nodded in the direction of Roman, who was storming over to them, fury coating his face.

"What is going on?" Roman demanded, brandishing papers in his hands.

"Um, I need you to be more clear," Avery said,

sitting straighter in her chair. "Roman, we're just talking. Beckett and I –"

"This isn't about Beckett. This about you. Or should I say about your twin sister, Ruby, the one who was actually supposed to be on the show."

He could have thrown a bucket of ice water on her for how her blood seemed to chill at his words. Beckett let out a long low whistle.

"Roman, I can explain –" Avery said, standing up and reaching out to him. He took a step back, disgust on his face.

"I can't stand liars."

"It wasn't like that. I've been honest about everything about who I am," Avery said.

"Except for your name – oh, and the fact that you aren't Ruby?"

"She begged me to take her spot for her. I shouldn't have listened to her, but I always seem to end up bailing her out. Please, Roman, you have to understand. She was worried she'd get sued by the show for pulling out last minute. It seemed harmless, all I had to do was tell people to call me Avery. I didn't lie about anything else, I promise. Every word I said was true," Avery pleaded, trying to make him understand her vantage point.

"All I see here is fraud," Roman spat. "And if you think you'll get the prize money just handed off to you now, you are dead wrong." Roman turned to walk away and Avery lunged at him, grabbing his arm and forcing him to stop.

"I don't care about the money, Roman. You don't have to give it to me. I need you to listen to me – please hear me out. My sister has a long history of getting herself into these situations and I always – *always* – bail her out. I wasn't going to help her this time, but I knew she was right about one thing. I had been hiding under a rock since my accident. I needed to be pushed – and god, was this a massive push, but I did it. I never meant to hide this from you."

"You could have told me," Roman bit out. "I thought we had something."

"Roman, we do. I almost did the other day but then the rainstorm came," Avery said, and saw Roman's gaze dip to her necklace and then back up to her face. "Please, Roman, please don't leave things like this with us. I want…"

"What do you want, Avery?"

"I want to spend more time with you. I think about you too, a lot. I want to give this an honest chance. I don't want to live a lonely life, sheltered in my apartment, hiding out from the big scary world. I want to take risks again. I want to travel the world with you and help make a difference. I have so many ideas on what we could do – how we could help. I want to give this a chance – give us a chance. Will you take that chance with me?"

Roman looked at her for an interminably long time before shaking his head no, crushing her heart with one look.

"I can't trust you. I'm sorry, Avery. You're not who you said you were."

With that, he disappeared into the villa.

Avery collapsed back onto the lounge chair, hugging her knees into her chest, and blinking through the tears that clouded her vision.

"He's just mad, Avery," Beckett said, coming to sit next to her and throwing an arm over her shoulder. "You can fix this. We have fragile egos, us men. Let his temper cool and it'll be okay."

"I don't think it will," Avery said, knowing Roman didn't trust easily – not with his background.

"Then he doesn't deserve you anyway. Relationships are going to have misunderstandings and arguments. If he can't get over this and work through it, then you can do better. Because you're pretty awesome, even if you pulled a fast one to get on the show."

"I didn't lie about who I was... not as a person," Avery promised. "It was just my name."

"I get that. And I kind of like that you did it. It's spunky. I like spunk."

"Well, look where I ended up."

"Exactly where you need to be. Now, tell me about this sister of yours... is she as hot as you?"

"Beckett," Avery warned.

"Kidding, kidding. I'm going after Cherylynn, don't you worry."

"You'd better, or I'll hunt you down and kick your butt."

"See? Spunky. I dig this Avery."

"I think I do too." Avery sighed and looked toward the villa, wondering how long she'd have to give Roman to cool down before she could make him see sense again.

CHAPTER 36

*S*ix *Weeks Later…*

"Dude, you need to chill," Luke, Roman's friend and cameraman, dropped to the ground next to Roman and leaned his back against a tree. They were in Liberia, producing a documentary on the black-market chimpanzee trade, and Roman had been working non-stop. He was at the point of exhaustion, but he didn't really care. All he wanted to do was keep working so he could drown out the vision of Avery's haunted eyes as she begged him to give her a chance.

"I am chill," Roman pointed out. A baby chimp snuggled into his chest under his shirt, skin to skin, which was about as chill as he thought he could get in this moment. They were staying at a rescue started by a couple from the States who had been doing their best to raise awareness as well as save the chimps. This particular chimp's mom had been stolen from him, and he needed round-the-clock care. Roman was currently on cuddle duty while the handlers took a little break. "I don't think it gets more chill than holding a baby chimp on my chest and sitting against a tree in the morning breeze."

"That's not what I'm talking about. When are you going to talk to her?"

Roman didn't have to ask who Luke was talking about. His friend had been on the show with them; he had been the one to deal with Roman's wrath when he'd been about to issue the bank transfer for the prize money and discovered Avery was not who she'd said she was.

"I've said all I need to say."

"I don't think you have," Luke said.

"Pretty sure I did."

"Pretty sure you didn't."

"Luke," Roman began, then shifted and wrapped his arm tighter around the snuggling chimp, "what else could I possibly have to say?"

"Um, maybe tell her that you love her?"

"What? That's crazy," Roman said. The chimp started awake at his words, blinking big eyes up at him, and then began to pick at Roman's chest hair. Roman shifted again and began doing the same back with the chimp's fur. Performing necessary grooming was a way to show love and care between chimps, and Roman was pleased to see the baby chimp picking up on the skills.

"You wouldn't be driving yourself – and your crew, mind you – into the ground if you didn't love her," Luke pointed out.

"Awww, am I working you too hard, pretty boy?" Roman asked, spoiling for a fight.

"Don't needle me just because you're heartbroken," Luke said. "You can hardly pick a fight when you've got a baby chimp on your chest. Talk to me, Roman. I'm your best friend. Why can't you let this go?"

"She lied to me. I can't get past that."

"She lied to the *show*. Not to you."

"A lie is a lie."

"Not all lies are made the same."

"My dad lied to my mom," Roman said, looking down at the chimp, not up at Luke. "He was married. A different life. A different person. He didn't tell her."

"Ah, there it is."

"Yeah, there it is."

"Avery's not your dad, though. She didn't deliberately mislead you. I don't think she went on the show thinking to find you there. To even find love. She was bailing her sister out, which speaks a lot to her sense of loyalty."

Roman hadn't let himself think like that.

"I don't think the show would have actually sued Ruby."

"They didn't know that. And it sounds like Avery has been buried in medical bills. I can see why the cash prize would be appealing to someone who can't get ahead of their debt."

"How do you know that?"

"I talked to the sister – Ruby. She was calling and calling, furious at you."

"She was?"

"She was. Do you know the last boyfriend left Avery too? When it got too tough?"

"I didn't leave Avery. And I'm not her boyfriend."

"You most certainly did leave her. Things got too tough and you left," Luke said. "You could've hashed it out then and there, but you let your pride get to you."

"She lied, Luke."

"Yeah, she made a mistake. People fuck up all the time. You can't tell me you're perfect. When will you learn to forgive?"

Roman just shrugged, not sure how to answer.

"Do me a favor, will you? I made something for you. Watch it when you go back to your room. Today."

"Maybe."

"I'm invoking the best friend clause. Promise me."

"Fine," Roman said, running his hand over the chimp's head. "I'll watch it."

"Good." Luke stood and looked down at him, "Why did you still give her the prize money if you were so mad at her?"

Roman shrugged again and looked away.

"Yeah, that's what I thought."

The chimp squealed against his chest, bouncing up and down as he did whenever his handler approached. Handing the happy baby off, Roman stood and stretched, then wandered toward his room. There he found his laptop open on his bed with a note from Luke.

Press play.

"Great," Roman said, plopping down on the bed and

pulling the laptop onto his lap. He hit the play button, then watched as Avery's beautiful face filled the screen. His heart swelled in his chest. She had no idea how lovely she was, Roman thought, his eyes drinking her in.

Despite his work obligations, he'd handed the tapes off to his editors and hadn't looked at anything from the show in weeks. But when his own face filled the screen, Roman realized this wasn't the edited copy of the show. His heart seized as he watched Avery stealing looks at him across the villa. The camera cut away to him interviewing her, and how he watched her when she walked away. To the night he had followed her into the water at the beach, when the siren had sung for them. And then to the day he'd rescued her, the look of sheer terror on his face bringing it all crashing back like a brick smashing through a window.

Luke had been filming them all along. He had compiled an entire video of Roman and Avery falling in love. Finally, it faded to black and words filled the screen.

What are you going to do about it?

EPILOGUE

*S*he'd taken a sabbatical from work.

Not that this was the time to take off from work, not when she didn't know what she wanted from her future – but Avery had worked relentlessly for years, never taking a holiday, and even her boss could see she was on the brink of burning out.

"Take three months," her boss had urged. "Think about what you want. We can use you on projects all over the world. Or maybe you'd like to propose something to us?"

"I can't just leave," Avery had protested.

Her boss had smiled at her, his eyes kind. "We actually care about our employees, Avery. You're about to burn out. I'd rather have you take the time and come back refreshed than have you implode on the job."

"But doesn't that reflect poorly on me?" Avery asked.

"How? We all need mental health breaks. We give

new parents leave to be with their newborns. We give people sick leave. Bereavement time. It's all a part of life. You can't ignore the human aspect of having employees. I've found over the years that we've had less turnover, and happier employees, when we just give people a chance to be human. Take the time, please."

Avery had taken the time. The prize money had come through, much to her shock, and she'd been able to clear her debt and put a nice chunk away in her savings. A part of her felt guilty for taking the money.

"Don't you dare give that money back, Avery," Cherylynn had threatened, having been debriefed on the whole story by Beckett. She'd breezed right past Avery's lie, saying she knew good character when she saw it, and had immediately launched into berating Roman for leaving Avery.

"It stills feels like I shouldn't have taken it," Avery said, still feeling guilty about the money. She jumped when Ruby smacked her hand on the table.

"Enough of that. What's done is done," Ruby said, turning on her lounge chair.

"She's right, you know," Cherylynn said, on the other side of Avery. The three of them had taken a holiday at the Laughing Mermaid. Ruby had left her world trip, claiming that Zane bored her, but Avery knew it was because she was worried about her sister. Cherylynn had wanted in on the girls' trip, and before Avery knew it, she'd found herself back on Siren Island, surrounded by a fierce group of powerful women, all of

whom were enjoying spending their time picking apart
Roman's bad decision.

"It's not like it was Roman's money. It was the
show's money. And let me tell you, honey, they are
going to profit so much from you. Do you have any idea
how much money these shows make? A hundred thousand dollars is nothing to them. Nothing at all. Consider
it being paid well for your appearance on television.
They owe you – especially since you weren't using the
show to build your brand like the other girls were."

"I hadn't thought about it like that," Avery admitted.

"Well, start. Jeez, I'm sick of this moping around,"
Cherylynn said. "What's done is done. You better get
back in the saddle soon, or I'm going to put your butt
there myself if I have to."

"We could go out dancing tonight," Mirra offered.

Cherylynn cheered. "Yes, dancing! Slutty clothes.
Hot island guys. Let's do it."

"Beckett won't like that," Avery smiled.

"He knows I won't touch another man. But just
because I'm on a diet doesn't mean I can't look at the
menu, honey."

"I'm not on a diet," Ruby pointed out. "I can eat *all*
the food."

"Smorgasbord," Cherylynn agreed.

Avery found herself laughing at them. Each day she
was getting a little better. It certainly helped to be
around such strong women – not to mention magical
ones. Now that she knew about the mermaids, Mirra and
Jolie had snuck her from her room several times at night

and had swum with her in the dark water in their mermaid form, slowly helping her to heal from her trauma. She'd even started snorkeling again – though never without a life jacket – and was slowly falling in love with all the beautiful fish that danced through the water.

"Avery," Irma said from the top of the path, "you have a visitor."

"I do?" Avery said, sitting up a bit.

Roman walked out in front of Irma. She patted him on the shoulder, as though to wish him good luck, and stepped back. The women all sat up and crossed their arms over their chests, and Roman walked down the path and into the lion's den.

"Well, well, well – look what the cat dragged in," Cherylynn said, examining her manicure. "Have you finally realized what a jerk you've been?"

"Cherylynn," Avery choked.

"I hope he has." Ruby stood and blocked Roman's path, looking up at him. "I'm Ruby, Avery's sister."

"I can see that," Roman said, looking between the identical twins. "It's nice to finally meet you."

"I can't say the same of you," Ruby said, disdain crossing her features while Avery buried her face in her palms. "But I hope you'll change my opinion of you."

"I plan to. If you'll let me pass, that is…" Roman said.

Ruby nodded, stepping back so he could walk over to Avery.

"Avery, may I speak with you?"

"I…"

"Come on, girls. I think we need to help with dinner," Jolie said. Quietly they all vacated the garden, leaving Avery on the lounge chair, her heart in her throat.

"Avery…" Roman said, sitting down beside her. "Will you look at me?"

"I can't believe you're here," Avery said, dropping her hands and looking down at her legs. Emotions whirled in her stomach and she wasn't sure if she was angry, sad, or happy.

"I shouldn't have left you, Avery. Not like that," Roman said. Reaching out, he danced his fingers over her hand until she turned it over, and he intertwined his fingers with hers.

"Why did you?" Avery asked, finally looking up to meet his eyes.

It all crashed into her. She'd missed him so much, and it hurt being this close to him again, not knowing what their future held.

"I… well, I'm an idiot," Roman began.

From the house, Cherylynn whooped. "You sure are!"

"Thank you very much, Cherylynn," Roman called. He tugged Avery up from the chair. "Can we walk?"

"Yes, probably best," she said, biting back a smile despite all the emotions that warred inside.

"Remember me telling you how my mom raised me? On her own?" Roman asked when they got to the beach and began to walk.

"I do, yes."

"Well, that's because my father, great guy that he was, lied to her. About who he was. He had a wife and kids at home. He strung her along until she got pregnant, then he freaked out and left. When… when I found out you weren't who you said you were, I lost it."

"Oh, Roman." Avery turned and pressed a hand to his chest. "I'm so sorry. I had no idea."

"I should have told you then. But, well, I'm a bit stubborn, you see."

"I do see that. You hurt me, you know, when you left. You really hurt me."

"I know I did," he said. "And I'm sorry for that. I'm here to ask if you'll let me make it up to you. You did promise you'd let me take you on a real date. Would you give me a chance again?"

"I…" Avery lost herself in his eyes for a moment. "I'd like to. I'm scared, though."

"The Avery I know was pretty fearless," Roman said, stepping closer so just an inch separated them. "The Avery I know ran into dark water in the night after a siren's song. The Avery I know helped bandage her wounded friend in the wild. The Avery I know stepped in and helped her sister in a bind, even though it meant getting on a tiny plane and traveling across the ocean. The Avery I know healed herself from a traumatic accident and started her life over. The Avery I know got right back on a kayak and paddled like she'd never paddled in her life. The Avery I know isn't scared of love."

Seeing herself in his eyes, Avery swallowed and nodded, tears rolling down her face.

"I like that Avery," she said.

"And I love her," Roman whispered. Then his lips were on hers, claiming her as his own.

Cheers rose from the villa and Avery stumbled back a step, laughing as she turned in Roman's arms to see her friends jumping up and down on the beach.

"They're impossible."

"And amazing. Sirens, every last one of them."

AFTERWORD

Unsurprisingly, I spend a lot of time underwater because I moved to the Caribbean to do just that. I have a very deep love for scuba-diving, and when I'm not writing I like to disappear into the ocean to take joy in the beauty that can be found there. I'm passionate about the conservation of coral reefs, and I love sharing this passion with my readers – both through my books and my scuba-diving photos that I share. I think a part of me has always dreamed of being a mermaid, as being underwater is a soothing and meditative experience for me. I hope my love for the ocean, my belief in the mystical, and my hope that fairy tales really can come true rings through for you in my books. Thanks for taking a peek into my world with me.

Would you like to visit the islands?

I have lovingly put together a free "Mermaid View" book with my own underwater photography. I took these photographs while diving, and the book is full of color and joy so download it to your computer, color tablet or phone. The bigger the screen the better it will look. I will also send you occasional emails with more Island Life photos along with updates on my newest books. I hope you enjoy the photos as much as I enjoyed taking them. Sparkle on, Sirens!

Download your free copy of 'Mermaid View'

https://offer.triciaomalley.com/88v21p6s0i

Be prepared to dive into a magickal realm where maybe...just maybe...once in a blue moon a mermaid finds her mate.

Book 4 in the Siren Island Series today.

Sign up for information on new releases, free books, and fun giveaways at my website
www.triciaomalley.com

CHAPTER 1

"*W*hat's with you today?"

"What do you mean?" Jolie caught the other side of the fitted sheet Mirra tossed to her, and together they made up the bed for the new arrival to the Laughing Mermaid. It was their slow season, as summers tended to be just short of unbearable with the heat, and they were pleased to have a long-term booking for one of their rooms.

"Your aura is off. Did you not sleep well?"

"My aura is fine, Mirra. Like you can even see auras. I think you're making it up." Jolie was constantly miffed that her and Mirra's magicks had manifested differently.

Like being mermaid wasn't magick enough?

It rankled when Mirra would flit around and diagnose people's ailments or personalities based on their aura colors. And most annoying of all was the fact that Mirra was more often right than wrong.

"You always say that. Jealous much? I don't say anything about your healing powers."

"That's because you're a healer too."

"Not as good as you are, Jolie, and you know it. Now, tell me what's bothering you." Mirra's beautiful face creased in concern as she studied her sister. Though they were born twins, they were anything but identical except for the fact that they were both breathtakingly beautiful. Mirra, light to Jolie's dark, was blond, ethereal, and soft of heart. Jolie, with her riot of dark curls, sharp blue eyes, and salacious wit, could cut through most men with a look and make them drop to their knees and beg. Mirra preferred a gentler approach; her men were often found composing poetry and planning romantic picnics. Jolie preferred the more rough-and-tumble types, and was just as happy wrapping her legs around a man in leathers on a motorcycle as she was sneaking into the captain's quarters on a ship. As sisters, they were yin to each other's yang, and a deep love abided between the two. When Mirra expressed concern, Jolie did her best to listen.

"I don't know…" Jolie shrugged, smoothing a duvet, brilliant green shot through with white threads, on the foot of the bed. "I'm just off today."

"Did you have bad dreams again?"

"Well, not the same one. A different one this time, actually."

"Tell me," Mirra said, moving to the sideboard to unload the basket of supplies they used to stock the rooms. Fresh fruit for the basket on the table, waters for the mini-fridge, tea and coffee by the kettle. They moved automatically, having done this change-over many times, and it soothed Jolie to work while she talked.

"This dream was about Irmine. About the night she lost him."

"Ah. That's an old one."

"It is."

"Why do you think it's come back now?"

"For me it feels like the dream focuses on the anguish of her loss and then her determination to make something of her life. It doesn't just end on the night she lost him, but skips ahead to how she's used that love to grow other areas of her life."

"So… a lesson then? How pain can lead to good?"

"Or maybe that we should still take a chance on love? Even if we can't know what the future will hold."

"I like that interpretation. It's more along the lines of how I like to think." Mirra, ever the optimist, beamed at Jolie.

"I know, which is why I'm surprised I'm thinking it."

"Will you look for love then?"

It was a constant discussion between the sisters. Their mother, Irma, had also lost their father tragically and had mourned him ever since. It had left the girls wary of deeper relationships – Jolie preferred to love 'em and leave 'em – but at the same time, their mother urged them to grab on and love as fiercely as they could.

Finding someone worthy of that love, however, was a whole different issue.

"Haven't I always?"

At that, Mirra let out a pretty peal of laughter, like the softest of bells chiming, and shook her head at Jolie.

"You most certainly have not. You've always looked for Mr. Right Now, and danced away from anything more serious. And plenty a man has wanted something more serious with you."

"I know." Jolie sighed, completely confident in her ability to ensnare men. "I haven't met the right man yet."

"How would you know? You barely give them a chance."

"O ye of the ol' aura readings... can't you tell? When you know, you know."

"I think you've grown bored and men come too easily to do your bidding. You need someone who'll stand up to you."

"I've dated plenty of bad boys," Jolie said, tying back the white linen curtains that framed the glass balcony doors. Beyond the doors, the sea called to her – like it always did, a primal pulse that beat deep in her soul – and Jolie took a moment to look out at the water.

"Bad boys that you could drop to their knees. You wrap every man around your finger. After a while, even that has to grow boring."

"I'll let you know when it does, darling."

"Shall we swim?" Mirra came to stand by her sister, and wrapped her arm around Jolie's waist. She knew the water soothed as much as it excited, and was always a surefire cure for whatever ailed them.

"Yes – the room's finished and everything else is touched up. I'll work out my angst in the water and then we can greet our delightful guest... what's his name again?"

"Dr. Theodore Macalister."

"Oh, a doctor? Sounds perfect for you, Mirra."

"You know the rules..." Mirra shot Jolie a look of censure over her shoulder.

"Right, right, don't sleep with the guests. Got it."

"Do you? Because Mom didn't make that rule because of me."

"Well, it was in place long before I shagged anyone here, so it's not because I broke it."

"No! You don't think –" Mirra gasped, turning on the staircase to laugh up at Jolie.

"Mirra! Of course! You can't think she's been celibate since our father died, can you?"

"I'd prefer not to think of it at all, really," Mirra said, a faint blush tinging her cheeks.

"Neither do I."

"Well, she may have grieved our father's death, but the woman is still living. And I'm sure she has her own needs, despite what you may think about those."

"You've got a good heart, Mirra. Much better than my cold and black one." Jolie laughed and bounced down the last couple of steps. "Let's go to the water. The call is particularly strong today."

"To the water then," Mirra agreed – but the concern didn't leave her voice.

Good Moon Rising by Tricia O'Malley
Available in audio, e-book, Kindle Unlimited &
paperback from Amazon.

I HOPE my books have added a little magick into your life. If you have a moment to add some to my day, you can help by telling your friends and leaving a review. Word-of-mouth is the most powerful way to share my stories. Thank you.

Ms. Bitch

"Ms. Bitch is sunshine in a book! An uplifting story of fighting your way through heartbreak and making your own version of happily-ever-after."

~Ann Charles, USA Today Bestselling Author

One Way Ticket

A funny and captivating beach read where booking a one-way ticket to paradise means starting over, letting go, and taking a chance on love…one more time

10 out of 10 - The BookLife Prize

Firebird Award Winner

Pencraft Book of the year 2021

CONTACT ME

I hope my books have added a little magick into your life. If you have a moment to add some to my day, you can help by telling your friends and leaving a review. Word-of-mouth is the most powerful way to share my stories. Thank you.

Love books? What about fun giveaways? Nope? Okay, can I entice you with underwater photos and cute dogs? Let's stay friends, receive my emails and contact me by signing up at my website

www.triciaomalley.com

Or find me on Facebook and Instagram.
@triciaomalleyauthor

Author's Acknowledgement

A very deep and heartfelt *thank you* goes to those in my life who have continued to support me on this wonderful journey of being an author. At times, this job can be very stressful, however, I'm grateful to have the sounding board of my friends who help me through the trickier moments of self-doubt. An extra-special thanks goes to The Scotsman, who is my number one supporter and always manages to make me smile.

Please know that every book I write is a part of me, and I hope you feel the love that I put into my stories. Without my readers, my work means nothing, and I am grateful that you all are willing to share your valuable time with the worlds I create. I hope each book brings a smile to your face and for just a moment it gives you a much-needed escape.

Slainté, Tricia O'Malley